TRAINING THE
ALPHA

I0620902

VIVIENNE SAVAGE

Names, characters, places, and incidents are the product of the author's imaginations or are used in a fictitious manner. Any resemblance to real persons, events, and locations are coincidental or used in a form of parody.

This is a limited edition collection.

Payne
&
Taylor
Publishing

ISBN-13: 978-0692491317

ISBN-10: 0692491317

CHAPTER 1

~THOMAS~

As I stirred awake and alone in my bed, my exhausted mind clung to the fading remnants of my dreams. Lips at my throat, a warm body nestled at my side, silken strands beneath my fingers. My eyes opened and the dream goddess evaporated like smoke, a ghost who only visited in my deepest sleep.

Ceres, my best and closest friend, was the girl I could never have. As fate would have it, she was also the girl I would always want, ever since the day my wolf had recognized her as our soulmate. It had been bittersweet irony that hers didn't see me, too.

To begin my day, I stumbled out of bed and I jolted myself awake under cold water while coffee brewed in the kitchen. Maybe I'm not a morning person, but the same can't be said for the woman sharing my house. Ceres is a dynamic force to be reckoned with — the kind of girl who would pop out of bed like bread from the toaster with her makeup all in place. She sets our coffee brewer each night, and if

I don't respond to the persistent ringing from the alarm clock she personally comes to shake me from bed.

Ceres lives with me out of convenience, a mutually beneficial arrangement until she gets her ass out of veterinary school. Her choice of future career is nothing short of hilarious considering what we are.

I was born human, but after we hit it off as pals and our friendship lasted through the rigors of pre-pubescent elementary school, her parents became threatened by my humanity. When they decided to move her across the city to separate us, Ceres had a simple solution. She bit me under the full moon, and I became her family's responsibility to train or kill.

Her dad Argus is a cool dude on top of being our pack leader. He and Ceres taught me to control my shifting until I could perform on a whim. Eventually I learned to resist the lure of La Luna, the moon goddess who guides our gifts, and once her father approved of me I became an honorary member of the family *and* the pack.

After tossing on jeans and a t-shirt, I ran my fingers through my towel-dried brown hair and exited the steamy bathroom to face my day. The aroma of strong coffee lured me like a siren's call into the small kitchen. I surrendered to habit and checked the line for voice mail from my renters. They never seemed to have complaints, but my grandfather instilled the morning and evening ritual in me.

"You're picking up a little weight, Tommy."

"What?" I spun from where I stood at the counter.

Ceres lounged at the dining table in her pajamas — a teal striped camisole and matching shorts barely covered her round bottom. Her demure smile warmed my blood. Because we were shifters, nudity wasn't new to us and I've been seeing her naked since our teens. Skimpy clothes and sensual outfits turned me on. I liked seeing girls in lace and lingerie.

"The good kind, I mean. Did you start working out again?" she asked.

I shook my head. "Naw. I run at night when I can sneak in an hour and I'm doing some work on the floors in Mrs. Drake's kitchen. I wish I had time for the gym." Relief flooded me and calmed my nerves. I felt silly that her opinion agitated me, my self-conscious mind the product of school-age teasing. Mentally, I'd always be the fat kid to some degree, no matter how many chicks checked me out now.

"Keep it up and you'll have bigger muscles than Craig soon."

My elation popped like a cheap balloon.

I muttered an unintelligible response and poured my coffee. Honestly, punching Craig in the face would be better than accepting we're alike in any way.

The optimist in me hoped Ceres would realize the man she needed was me, but at this point, I'd settle for her just finding a man who appreciated her. A man who didn't talk shit to her in public, who didn't embarrass her for the boys, and loved her as much as she deserved. In the meantime, she goes for rich bad boy with a killer smile and prestigious role on the football team. The guy who's going to dick her and leave.

"Have a good day at work, Tommy! Oh, wait! I packed a lunch for you!" She caught up to me in the foyer with a sack lunch. I smelled the chicken, bacon, and ranch through the Ziplock bag. My favorite.

"Sweet. Thanks. Good luck with your last clinical day."

With caffeine fueling me, I headed out for a busy shift on the phones as a tech support agent. Four days a week my schedule was shit, but it gave me a three-day weekend and time to handle jobs that cropped up in the houses I owned. When my grandparents died, our relatives came out of the woodwork each demanding their fair share of my grandparents' holdings. Since my dad had died serving in the Army, my uncle expected to receive all of them in the will.

Had any of them visited during Gramps' final days? Helped change the man's diapers after he'd had a stroke? No, *this* guy did, and it was an act out of love for a man I respected my whole life, not a scam to become the sole heir in the will. So, instead of spitting on their gift, I honored their last wishes and tried to keep all the property in our family. I kept up with their renters, honored their lease agreements, and told my Uncle Todd to kiss my ass by firing him to hire another property manager.

Shortly after Gramps passed away, Ceres came to me in a jam. The decision to allow her to move in seemed like a good idea at the time. Argus and Vesta thought I'd rub off on her some.

A quiet home was a welcome blessing when I returned at the end of the day to our residential street in rural Atropos, Texas, population 2,038. Without stopping by the fridge for an afternoon snack, I headed upstairs and collapsed on the sofa in our sitting parlor. Ceres showed up an hour later wearing her white lab coat.

"Good day?" I asked as she trudged by.

"Yeah. I'm glad I chose small animal care over equine medicine now. Horses are assholes," she muttered as she hung up her coat. "I spent all day busting ass because someone overbooked, but I wanted to end the final day with a good impression."

"Good. Maybe someone will appreciate it enough to give a reference when you do decide on a residency program. Or they'll pick you up there."

"That's my hope." She flashed me a cheery smile and stepped toward her bedroom door. A mewling cry escaped her purse.

"Ceres... did your fancy handbag just meow at me?"

She stopped, turned slowly, and looked at me with an abashed smile. "Busted."

Ceres unsnapped her Coach bag and pulled out a small, bedraggled kitten. Its striped orange coat was matted and dirty. Country road debris and filth glued one of its eyes shut.

"Two teenagers were trying to drown him in a ditch, Tommy... and I just couldn't leave the poor thing there. Look at him."

"Trying to drown him?" I sat up a little straighter in my seat.

"Yeah. I took their photo with my cell phone and said I'd call the sheriff's department if they didn't give him to me and leave."

"You should still report them. Animal cruelty is jailable now."

"Okay, I will but... can we keep him, Tommy? Please?"

"Are you serious?" When it came to animals, I preferred dogs for the obvious reasons.

"Tommy, please."

"I don't know… Right now, you're the worst roommate ever." Okay, far from being the worst roommate ever, but I wasn't above poking fun at her when the situation warranted it.

"I'll take care of him, I swear. He won't be a bother. I'll jog to the Dollar Shoppe right now and get him the basics."

Her begging and pleading worked. Ceres left the little fuzzball in my lap and dashed back out. Shivering, it gazed up at me and sneezed.

A little under an hour later, she returned with an armload of basic supplies. We scrubbed him in her bathtub, she blow-dried him, and then I dumped a bowl of soft cat food while she prepared the other essentials.

Ceres stepped into view and smiled at me. She hadn't changed her clothes, so her damp camisole revealed the lacy outline of a pale pink bra. Being a shifter had normalized nudity to the point where I'd latch on to anything to sexualize the female body again. Even if it was only a damned satin bow on a bra strap. "Thank you, Tom—"

"Don't thank me yet. You're paying me back for this one." She lived off her scholarships and grants, while her parents paid most of her tuition.

"I know, Tommy. I will. But just look at him, sleeping so peacefully." The kitten lay curled up on the couch beside me, oblivious to how much I would have preferred to find him another home. "Okay, I'm going to get cleaned up now."

"'Kay. I'll be right here."

Ceres kissed my cheek then went to her room.

For a few moments, I allowed myself to daydream. I imagined her clothes hitting the floor and the cling of her undergarments. My active imagination chose the lacy yellow panties Ceres left hanging to dry in our laundry room a few days ago.

"Hey! Earth to Thomas, are you listening to me?"

My attention snapped away from the television. Ceres waited with her hands on the hips of her low-rise jeans, standing seductively with her thumbs hooking into the belt loops. It revealed enough skin to earn a lingering stare before my reply. "Yeah?"

"I need a ride into San Antonio. Like now. Pleeeease," she begged me. Before I could decline with an excuse, she bent both knees and dipped, pressing both hands together in a gesture of prayer. "*Please?*"

Her smiles could melt ice, and I didn't have a chance once she turned one on me. My best friend, the oblivious object of my affection, had me wrapped around her finger. I rolled my eyes and dragged it out, pulling in a theatrical breath next, and then humming thoughtfully. "I don't know…"

"Tommy, please! You know I'll make it up to you when Mom and Dad finally give me my car back." She knelt down on the floor beside the couch and stroked her fingers lazily down the kitten's back, stretching her arm over my thigh to reach him. I agreed wholeheartedly with his purrs and wished she would stroke me instead.

"I dunno…"

"I'll do the dishes for a week."

Bingo. "You better mop the floors and clean the fridge, too," I told her, putting a big grin on my face.

"Fine." She jumped up to her feet.

"Where we goin'?" I asked. A me-shaped indentation remained in the seat when I stood, and my joints popped loudly. Ceres' nose wrinkled at the protesting sounds.

"I'm going to meet up with Craig at the movies." Craig is the current flavor of the school term and will probably be replaced by some other creep once she graduates. I always tell myself it's not my circus, and these aren't my monkeys. Minding my own business gets easier as time goes by.

The short drive into San Antonio takes about half an hour. Her verbally abusive boyfriend Craig is a typical jock without a future. He doesn't play ball well enough for a team to scout him. He'll graduate in a couple weeks with a useless Bachelor's degree in Nutrition and Food Studies. In a year, he'll be peddling protein powder to desperate people looking for a miracle diet.

"Thanks for the ride, Tommy. Craig's gonna bring me back."

Ceres kissed my cheek and left the cab of the pickup. Without a backward glance, she jogged to the asshole awaiting her and dragged him down into a kiss. A vicious stab of jealousy chiseled away another piece of my heart.

I'm forgotten already.

***

I've never regretted inviting Ceres into my home, but what I *do* regret is that she chose the bedroom above mine. Craig's grunts sound like a boar rutting at a sow, but her moans quickly aroused my own hunger. I hadn't had a girlfriend since dumping Susan before Christmas and getting her fingers out of my pockets.

The mattress yielded a final creak and silenced, indicating Craig finished first as usual. For the first time since entering her room, they quieted down for a verbal exchange too low for my keen ears to discern the words.

Eventually, once I resisted the temptation to phone Susan for a pity fuck, I fell into a difficult, uneasy sleep and spent the rest of the night in my tangled sheets.

When morning came, a few scattered rays of sunlight slipped through the wooden slats covering my window. I dragged myself out of bed and into the bathroom. Sometimes it took time for the ancient water heater to negate the chill, so I left it on full blast for a while to warm up as I made the bed.

To confirm his new purpose in life, the orange tabby snaked around my ankles, as if ready to trip me. Cats are evil clever bastards and this one was starting young, proving my theory they're just born that way. I shooed him out of the room and closed the door. He could go cry to Ceres for his morning food.

The foggy mirror greeted me when I re-entered the tidy and organized bathroom to strip down. According to Ceres, my flat stomach is the best trait of my lean physique, and I happen to agree with her there. My driver's license says I'm 6'1", but it's probably more like 6'2" since I'm working on my slouch. I've almost completely defeated that bad habit.

The hot water cascaded over me once I stepped beneath the steaming showerhead to wash away my worries. My relief didn't last for long when bigger problems haunted my thoughts, most of which concerned my dwindling personal finances.

I couldn't work for Ravensloft forever, and I certainly didn't plan to survive by living a couple dollars above the minimum wage. Fortunately, Ceres would be bringing in money again soon as a productive, employed member of society.

Ceres... Her name whispered through my thoughts, bringing with it the fantasies of her bedtime attire. Her tiny shorts, the off the shoulder tops, and the nightshirts that barely skimmed her ass.

About a half hour later, I emerged unshaven and scruffy.

"About time you came out, sleepyhead. I made ya some bacon," Ceres greeted me. Her green eyes twinkled. For one heart pounding second, I felt as if she understood how much I wanted and craved her.

Why didn't her wolf recognize mine?

"Thanks."

Ceres wore her ash blonde hair twisted into a sloppy updo, but a few strands escaped the bun to tickle her cheeks. An oversized fuchsia sweatshirt hung off her shoulders, revealing a nude bra strap. I impulsively adjusted it. Over the years, Ceres and I had acquired a certain kind of comfort with each other, courtesy of the friend zone. When we were teens, I squeezed her tits once and asked when she'd gotten a boob job, but she'd only laughed and playfully swatted my hands before kissing my cheek. It was as if she didn't see me as a man at all.

"Don't you have class today?" I asked. "It's kinda late in the semester to start skipping."

"Shush you. Yesterday was my last clinical day, remember? Beth is picking me up so we can go to some sort of exit ceremony they planned for our graduating class." She winked at me and poked my cheek with one finger. "Aren't you going to shave, or are you trying to resemble your wolf side while you're on two legs, too?"

"I shaved two days ago." Maneuvering around her to enter the kitchen, I was assaulted with the smell of buttery eggs and mouthwatering bacon. Ceres may be ignorant when it comes to men, but she used her skills in the kitchen like a weapon.

"The scruff suits you." She spooned scrambled eggs onto my plate next to the fried pork.

"Okay, what's up? You made breakfast, complimented me, and you haven't rushed out the door." I paused a second, granting her time to develop a genuinely confused expression. "Payday isn't until next Thursday if you planned to ask for a loan, and I already spent the rent money from my other tenants."

"What makes you think I need money?" Her tone was too sharp. I was spot on.

"You only cook for me when you want something in return."

"That is completely untrue," she grumbled. Ceres made a show of dishing up her own plate. Her jaw tightened, and the gears whirred in her head.

Approaching the issue from another angle, I craftily reworded my inquiry. "What do you need to buy?"

"It's nothing important."

"C'mon, Ceres. What do you need?"

"It was nothing, Tommy."

She said little else for the rest of breakfast, a silent, brooding woman opposite me at the table.

Thirty minutes later, I headed for the door, planning to jog around the block and enjoy the sun.

Miss Kent waited on the stoop with her hand raised to knock. Straight black hair framed her freckled, smiling face. She and her son Jamie lived beside us in one of my rental houses.

"Hey, Miss Kent."

"Emma's fine. You know, like I told you the last dozen times." When she grinned, her cheeks dimpled and made her look too young to be a mother.

Trying to shuck off the old habits drilled into me by my grandfather, I smiled and nodded. "Emma." My eyes drifted down to the boy at her side. "What about you, Jamie? No school today?"

"Nope." Jamie was a good kid, and as far as I knew, his dad wasn't in the picture at all. He was darker in skin tone than his mom, but they both shared the same brown eyes. Jamie had half of her Native American blood. Potawatomi, I think. Jamie was already inching up on Emma's short height and I figured in another two years he'd tower over his mom.

"So, what can I help you with? Is something broken?"

"No, no, nothing like that. I made a huge batch of chili last night. More than Jamie and I can eat, anyway. Guess I got overly ambitious with my new slow cooker." She laughed and tucked her hair behind her ear. "I was wondering if you'd like some."

"Oh." Emma sold baked sweets in the local cafe, using me often as a happy test subject for her new recipes. She'd never offered me an actual meal before. "Sure, I'd love that. Thanks."

"Great. I'll drop some off after Jamie's doctor appointment. Okay?"

"Sounds good. Y'all drive safe now." I ruffled Jamie's curly hair and received a small but tired smile in return. Poor kid. Asthma was kicking his ass lately.

My sympathy for Jamie didn't stop me from checking out Emma's behind when they walked away. She belonged to the same club as Kim Kardashian and Beyoncé — even a blind man could see that ass.

After I stepped outside into the balmy May air, I waved goodbye and tucked my earbuds in. A run was the perfect medicine to clear my head and help me devise a way to meet financial obligations over the long summer.

CHAPTER 2

~THOMAS~

"Oh yeah, baby, right there. Harder. Harder!"

Susan's bottom was her best attribute, showcased by the bent position, giving me a perfect view. My ex-girlfriend liked sex hard and fast along with a lot of dirty talk. Sex had never been our issue. Her conniving ways and greedy tactics had even spurred Ceres, the High Maintenance Queen herself, into warily voicing a concern.

Susan's bountiful tits bounced and swung wildly to the frenetic tempo of my thrusts. I crashed my hips into her perfectly round ass again and again, impaling her on my hard prick. My gym shorts pooled around my ankles and her short summer dress was flipped around her waist, where it occasionally tickled my lower abs. We hadn't even bothered to strip down completely.

And to think I'd only entered her tiny apartment for a glass of water. My t-shirt clung to me, sticking against my shoulders and back. I'd feel miserable if I wasn't balls deep in a gorgeous girl, making her scream my name.

I gripped a handful of her dress and tugged downward, spilling her full breasts against my bare palms. Susan's tits were a little too perfect to be genuine, higher and perkier than possible for their size. To my wandering hands, they were as good as the real deal. I squeezed them roughly and teased one sensitive nipple between my index and middle digits. My other hand descended to tease the hot junction of our bodies by fingering her clit.

"God, Tommy. Don't stop, baby."

Susan had this thing she did — the kind of thing that made her pussy almost feel like a vice. I'd always imagined it was like fucking a tight little virgin, only there was nothing innocent about the things she'd done to me during our relationship.

"*Fuck*. If you do that again I won't have much choice," I gritted through my teeth.

"Do what? This?" She knew exactly what she was doing, squeezing her muscles around me in rhythmic pulses. "Come for me, Tommy, so we can fuck again. You always do it right."

In my head, I imagined Ceres bent in front of me, her insides massaging my cock with intimate spasms. My balls tightened, I groaned, and just like that, her body convulsed around me to provide a bittersweet, mutual orgasm. She wasn't the girl I wanted, but she'd given me what I needed. Sweat trickled down my back and a few clinging droplets fell from my hair to land against her flushed skin. Our fucking was never calm and quiet.

"Haven't you missed this?" she purred, gyrating her hips back against me. The enticing movement threatened to renew my hard-on.

Despite her efforts, I remained semi-hard, defiant to the very end. I shook my head and stepped away from her to clear my thoughts. It took only a second to haul my sweats and boxer briefs back into place after I tossed the used condom into the waste bin beside the bed.

"You're a great lay, Susan, but that's all it is. It's been over between us for a long time now." A conflict between my conscience and my dick meant I couldn't get her hopes up that this was a shot at reconciliation. I was already beginning to feel foolish for accepting her invitation inside.

"That's what you said the last time. You fucked me in your truck outside of school, remember?"

Mid-March, I'd foolishly answered a text from her on a dismal, rainy afternoon. Her ride had stranded her at college and she begged me to help. Susan had ended up straddling me before I even took the vehicle out of park. I blame the wet shirt she wore. Or maybe it was the skin-tight leggings she'd peeled off in the passenger seat as an excuse to get warm.

"Yeah, well... that shouldn't have happened either, Susan."

"It's that rich chick living in your place, isn't it?"

"It doesn't have anything to do with Ceres," I lied awkwardly. I didn't make eye contact. I'd always been a piss poor liar and after two years of dating, Susan saw through me.

"Geez. I always thought you had a thing for her, but you're really hung up on that bitch, aren't you?" She rolled over and pushed up on her elbows. Her casual sprawl drew my gaze down her bare legs. My cock twitched, but ultimately remained useless.

"Nobody needs a reason to dump you, Suse. Grow up. Maybe once you get your hands out of a man's pocket, he'll want to stay with you."

"Yeah, well, at least I rent my own place and don't mooch off my lovesick bestie." She flopped back against the pillows and made no effort to cover her sweat-sheened body. Content as a kitten, she lounged in the afterglow of our sex.

Her words stung more than I dared to let on.

"You know where to find me if you need me, Tommy, but I'm not going to wait on you. Fair warning."

I fucked her again with her face buried in the pillow to muffle her passionate cries. This time, the position and desired depth of my strokes had nothing to do with it. I didn't want to see her face. I didn't want to view the smug satisfaction when I made her come again.

Two years of verbal abuse, financial exploitation, and no true affection fueled my impulsive act of reprisal.

Her walls practically quivered around my hard length, her orgasm so close, yet just beyond her reach. A little twitch of my fingers against her clit would have hurled her over the edge, but I pulled out and ripped the condom off to blow my load on her ass. A wayward streak of cum landed in her sweat-dampened blonde curls. I wiped off on her right ass cheek and rose from my kneeling position behind her on the bed.

"Tommy?" Susan's startled voice called after me. Her breaths heaved, escaping in small pants. She'd been so close that I heard it in her voice. "Come back here."

"No thanks."

"What are you doing?" she hissed after me.

I removed my wallet and pulled two crumpled twenties from it. I tossed both on her before I turned away. "Paying my whore what she's worth. Goodbye, Susan."

A foul-mouthed string of epitaphs followed me to the door. Every word was worth it.

CHAPTER 3

~THOMAS~

My job leads me to believe most people online didn't deserve a computer. I spend most of my days at work talking people through common errors and asking questions like, "Have you recently updated your graphics driver?" Meanwhile, my good friend manages the floor and was the anchor that kept me at the company.

"Why don't you go ahead and clock out early, Tommy," Harrison said.

Harrison was one of my best pals and also the owner's son. He and Mr. Corbeau could have passed for brothers with their black hair and identical, boyish faces. His dad blamed his youthful appearance on his exercise regime but I know the real truth. The Corbeau family are shifters too, but not wolves like Ceres and me. They're ravens.

"What? And have some free hours to myself?"

My friend punched my shoulder. "I'm going to meet up with Darrell and Jameson at the bar, and I've decided to drag you with me since Bobby can't come. You've missed out on the last few."

"Is Jameson's band playing again or something?"

"Nah, he's off tonight. Just us, some steaks, and bottles of Shiner," Harrison replied.

The idea tempted me.

"Fuck yeah. I'd love to, man, but I promised Ceres I'd pick up dinner."

"Is she still living with you?"

"Yeah. Where else would she be?" I asked.

"Hot piece like that, I figured she'd be living with her boyfriend or something. What about that Brazilian soccer player dude? Are they still dating?" Harrison asked.

"Marcelo was last year's douche, man. She caught him with some blonde hottie in his apartment and dumped his ass after an epic catfight."

"Okay, then what's the deal with Susan? I ran into her in Walmart yesterday and when I mentioned your name…" Harrison whistled.

I rubbed the back of my neck and glanced away guiltily. After I caught Harrison up on the newest development in my relationship with Susan, his eyes practically bugged out of his head.

"You didn't. Dude, just tell me that you're joking."

"I did."

"*Why?*"

I asked myself the same question at least twice since storming out of her apartment. It seemed like a good idea at the time and a surefire way to break things permanently.

"She's a leech. Good sex doesn't make up for that," I said.

Harrison eyed me as if I'd lost my mind. Maybe I had since there were moments when Ceres didn't appear to be any better. "Whatever, man. Anyway, go, get your pizza."

"Thanks. Tell the guys I said 'sup."

After I logged my hours, I headed out into the late afternoon sunshine. The guys were right. Getting out of the house more would be great for me, but I'd looked forward to the time with Ceres. Besides, it'd take a real fool to count on her cooking after a week of finals.

I decided against pizza and stopped at Mrs. Mabel's Lazy Diner for a bucket of chicken then splurged on hard cider at the liquor store. Craig liked to spend Friday nights out with the frat brothers, which guaranteed an evening alone without his condescension.

"Ceres?"

Under normal circumstances, I'd cherish a silent house. Disappointment soured my mood instead, since I'd anticipated a night of action movies on the sofa beside Ceres. Craig must have changed his mind about guzzling cheap pisswater with the guys and dragged her along.

Chester, as she had affectionately named our new kitten, greeted me by rubbing his face against my ankle. I leaned down to pet him before I headed into the kitchen to set the cider and chicken on the dinette table. I glanced at his bowl in passing. Good. Ceres fed our little guy. The little jerk was growing on me.

Seconds after I hit start on a side dish of microwave macaroni and cheese, a noise from the

23

hallway's guest bathroom nearly scared me into an early grave. "Ceres?" I called again, suppressing the horror movie apprehension churning in my belly. If a knife-wielding lunatic burst into the hallway to kill me, I had no one to blame but myself for failing to acknowledge the signs.

Fortunately, that wasn't the case. The half-closed door afforded me a partial view within the brightly lit chamber. Ceres wore her favorite jeans again, denim hugging her curves in all the right places, worn thin and white just beneath the pockets.

The contents of her purse littered the vanity, strewn over the clean counter space.

"Are you going out?"

Ceres jerked and dropped the small cap balanced on her palm. Flesh-toned powder scattered across the counter and into the porcelain sink.

"Holy shit, Tommy, you scared me!"

"Sorry. I called, but I guess you didn't hear..." I stopped, my gaze locked on her reflection. Cold, unbridled fury seized me and chased away all my other thoughts. A hard nudge opened the door with a bang, slamming it against the wall. Ceres ducked her head and tried to hide her face behind her hair. Too late. I took her by the arm and whirled her around to face me.

"Did that asshole hit you?"

She tugged away from me, but my grip held firm. "It's... it's nothing, Tommy. I had too much to drink and walked into a door."

Bullshit. "What the fuck happened?" Her artful application of foundation and powder concealed about half of the shiner blooming around her left eye.

"I told you… C'mon, Tommy, I didn't want you to see me like this."

"The hell were you planning to do? Sleep in your makeup for a couple days?" I demanded.

"Maybe…"

A glitzy top clung to her upper body, exposing her shoulders. Ceres didn't have a lot of boob, but she knew how to dress to enhance her best attributes. She'd worn her shoes into the bathroom in her rush to hide the damage. Four-inch stilettos brought her up to my height, and we were nearly eye-to-eye.

"Fuck, he hit you hard as hell, didn't he? You put any ice on it yet?"

Instead of judging her or losing my cool, I applied water to a cloth and gently washed her face. Each tear she shed made me want to pound Craig's face in, so I fucking counted them. Every single silent drop. By the time I'd finished wiping away the makeup, I was a master of my emotions with a phony smile on my face as I gestured to the fried dinner on the dinette table.

"You up for a bite to eat?"

"Yeah… thanks."

I carried the goods to the second floor, balancing chicken on one hand and a pack of hard cider in the other. I'd shoved two spoons into the bowl of macaroni and clutched it awkwardly against me.

"You wanna talk about it?" I asked after we settled on the sofa.

She ignored my question and stuffed her face instead. We made the best of a shit situation with cooling chicken legs and warming hard cider. We watched movies, Ceres' head on my shoulder and blonde hair fanned down my t-shirt. I breathed in the

25

fresh scent of cucumber and melon in her wavy hair, held her close, and wished things were different.

We stretched along the couch and snuggled through an adventurous film featuring werewolves and vampires. The absurd depictions made us dissolve into fits of laughter. Chester abandoned us halfway through, annoyed we kept waking him from his nap on the armrest.

"Do you think I should get a boob job?" she asked. "Emma has big tits and they look great."

The absurd question took me out of the movie. "What the hell kinda question is that?"

"Well I'm right, aren't I?" Ceres twisted around to look at me. Something about my expression made her giggle. "Oh, c'mon Tommy, don't look so amazed. If I checked her out, I know for sure that you did."

Miss Kent's hourglass proportions had been the subject of conversation among some of the neighborhood men since she moved into town. "Erm... She's my tenant, Ceres. Anyway, what the hell makes you think you need to change?"

"I'm serious. There's space leftover in my B cup bras. Should I get a boob job once I'm working? You know, earning my own money?"

"Woman, what do you think is going to happen to those implants when you shift?"

She grimaced. "Good point."

"Besides, nobody needs more than a handful. I mean, it's nice, but you don't *need* it."

Her slender fingers slid over my left hand and raised it away from my thigh. She brought it over to her left breast and molded the palm over her tit. She hadn't worn a bra beneath the fancy summer top, the thin material under my palm failing to disguise that her nipple had tensed.

"I guess I do have a handful."

Even with two layers of denim between us, I was sure she could feel my stiffening cock against her ass. My noncommittal grunt provoked her to continue, squeezing my fingers tighter until I kneaded her breast. Despite its small size, it was plump in my hand. I took her cue and squeezed the other breast too then teased the nipple until it hardened.

"You're fine. Your tits are great the way they are. Don't ruin 'em with implants."

"Okay, Tommy." She peeked at me and smiled.

We watched the rest of the movie that way, trading touches like teenagers and occasionally sneaking subtle sniffs. Around midnight, I realized she'd fallen asleep. She snuggled against me and turned her face against my throat, beckoning me with the honey-cider sweetening her breath and parted lips. My friend even teased and tempted me in her sleep. I risked stroking her hair away from her face then skimmed the curve of her ear and traced down her throat.

Then her lips touched my skin. At first, I thought it was her shifting again in her sleep, but then her hand slid up my chest and her kiss firmed. Ceres nestled upon me, sliding over my lap into a straddling position.

I dove headfirst into the moment without speaking a word, petrified I'd shatter the dream and wake up to a raging morning hard-on until I stroked off in the shower. Ceres fit in my lap perfectly. She belonged there, and I'd needed her for so long. With my hands sliding down her back to her ass, I nudged my hips upward to show her exactly what she did to me.

Her breathy gasp was a reward all its own. And it got even better.

Ceres unzipped my jeans and boldly drew my cock through the opening. Before I could utter a word of surprise, she curled her fingers and pumped the length in her hand. Her fingertips barely touched. She slipped her thumb over the sensitive head, smearing the clear drop of precum on the tip.

"Ceres…"

She silenced me with a finger to my lips and another pistoned stroke of her hand.

I accidentally popped one of the strings on her glitzy top, too eager to realize it unfastened behind the shoulder. Without a bra in my way, I squeezed both tits and kissed her hard. Cider flavored her tongue and laced every kiss, while her responsive body writhed beneath my attentive touches. I pinched her nipples until they stiffened and tore my mouth away from her lips to suck one pink tip. She expressed her pleasure with a throaty moan.

I had to get inside her. If her fingers were this good I could only imagine how right her body would feel surrounding my dick, gliding up and down. My fingers dealt with the button on her jeans and I bumped her up with my hips until she was on her feet.

"These need to go." I ripped the frayed denim down her legs and pulled her panties down next, revealing bald skin. It was freshly waxed, a smooth plane for me to explore with my tongue. Without hesitation, I leaned in and kissed the sensitive flesh, my hands holding her steady at her hips. She threaded her fingers through my hair and tilted her head back, moaning.

The wolf in me demanded the chance to claim her for a mate, but the man in me wanted to make love to my best friend.

"Do we need a condom?"

"Tommy… Tommy, no." A backward step took her out of my reach.

"Do we?" Usually wolves couldn't conceive until a female was in heat. Ceres definitely wasn't, but she'd know better than me.

"Wait, Tommy, okay? Maybe this… this was a bad idea. I don't want… to make a mistake." Ceres pulled her panties up without making eye contact with me then plucked her top from the floor to hold it over her breasts.

"Now, you're changing your mind because I asked a question? What the fuck, Ceres?"

"I'm sorry," she cried. "But… it's *you* and this… We shouldn't do this, Tommy."

"Me? What the hell is that supposed to mean? Why *not?*" I wished her rejection could have soothed the erection jutting from my crotch, but it didn't. The dull throb continued relentlessly.

"It's just… I mean… You're… you. Tommy. I just thought for a second that you'd…." She shook her head and retreated from me. "I don't know what I was thinking… why I even…" Her breath shuddered out. "Let's forget this happened. I'm gonna go to bed."

"Just like that?" I stared at her incredulously until pride finally took hold. Taking her cue, I looked away from her and tucked myself away into my boxers first. I zipped up and folded my arms against my chest.

"This feels like a mistake. I'm sorry." And just like that, she scurried off to her room. The half-open door was as much of a tease as the girl undressing again on the other side.

Grunting, I left my seat on the couch and abandoned the mess from dinner. I wanted to run. No, I needed to. I jerked clothes off as I went, leaving my top on the stairs and my jeans in the kitchen.

Pitch-black backyards were one of those things I loved about small town living — none of those godawful streetlights shining through windows. I took off at a run, cool grass beneath my bare feet, and let the shift take me. I can't even begin to describe how it feels. It hurts and liberates me at the same time, an agony that comes with its own reward. Every time my bones pop and snap, it's like destroying a small piece of me and setting my soul free. With four paws on the ground, I increased my speed and leapt over my low fence.

As a wolf, the world came alive in a whole new way. I was aware of everything around me: squirrels running up the trees, maple bourbon and bacon wafting from Miss Kent's open kitchen window, old man Keener's coon dogs down the street, and the hum of a dozen conversations from the houses behind me. Wanting to clear my head, I pushed on until I left all the human distractions behind.

There was a party going on at an abandoned farmhouse, which was easy enough to circle around without being seen. The mix of scents was nauseating to my sensitive nose. Body odor clashed with an overabundance of perfume and cheap cologne, sour beer, cigarette smoke, and much more. The smell didn't dissipate until I reached the woods.

I put on a burst of speed, determined to push Ceres out of my mind.

~CERES~

Everything I ever felt about Tommy changed in the span of a heartbeat. I knew his wolf had attuned to me, but a lifetime of friendship had passed without mine seeing him in return.

That was no longer true. Something white hot and brilliant spread through my soul, consuming me like fire until every nerve became awash with sensation and heat. The transition took place so swiftly and without warning that I was left breathless beneath him and struck senseless.

No, no, no. The wolf in me became a mad bitch in heat, desperate for him and absolutely aware of the power he possessed. I couldn't allow her to take me down an irreversible path until I had time to process the new change. Without a doubt, I knew the outcome of sex with Tommy would end with our bonding, and there'd be no possible way to return to the simple friendship between us.

"Do we need a condom?"

"Tommy... Tommy, no." With difficulty, I stepped out of his reach.

"Do we?"

God, his cock was so hard. I licked my lips nervously and darted my gaze to the door. "Wait, Tommy, okay? Maybe this... this was a bad idea. I don't want... to make a mistake." I couldn't face Tommy's disappointment. Like a coward, I dressed myself without looking at him. I needed time to think and mull over what was happening to us, happening to *me*.

"Now, you're changing your mind because I asked a question? What the fuck, Ceres?"

What? No! "I'm sorry," she cried. "But... it's *you* and this... We shouldn't do this, Tommy," I blubbered out the words. He was the last man I ever wanted to hurt. The only guy besides my dad who ever gave a damn about me.

"Me? What the hell is that supposed to mean? Why *not?*"

"It's just... I mean... You're... you. Tommy. I just thought for a second that you'd...." *Always be my best friend. The guy I could turn to when the chips were down. The funny, witty guy who could make me smile and laugh at the drop of a hat.* "I don't know what I was thinking... why I even... Let's forget this happened. I'm gonna go to bed."

"Just like that?" Tommy pulled his jeans back into place and shot me a betrayed look. He didn't force it the way Craig would have, a big difference between the man I dated and the friend who loved me because a shitty magical bond obligated him to feel this way.

"This feels like a mistake. I'm sorry." A mistake that, if made now, would change the dynamic of our relationship forever. I couldn't let one error in judgment ruin everything, so I ran away to my room and hid from him as turbulent feelings waged in my heart.

Mate with him, end our friendship, turn it into something else. Or step away now and know we could always be there for each other. Through my partially open door, I heard Tommy moving around, and part of me wished he'd rush into my room and assert his dominance like an alpha, telling me everything would be okay and would never change. He didn't, and he probably never would.

The back door opened and shut, slamming with a bang. All evidence pointed to the likelihood of Tommy spending the night on all fours, prowling the countryside.

With the lights out in my bedroom, I snuck to the window and peeked between the curtains to see his tall and lean wolf form sprinting across the grass. I longed to run with him, and if I were stronger, maybe I would have.

Maybe if I weren't so weak, I'd tell him that my wolf recognized his, too, but that I just needed a moment to think it through.

Drawing in a sharp inhale, I shut the curtains again and moved into the shower.

CHAPTER 4

~THOMAS~

Four strikes slammed against the front door. I groggily shambled out of bed in my underwear and stepped into the foyer. The sight through the peephole woke me up fast, and I yanked open the door. Craig's hand almost caught me in the face but I moved to the side and he staggered forward.

"Man, it's…" I glanced over my shoulder at the old cuckoo clock hanging on the wall. "It's almost five in the fucking morning. What do you want?" He reeked of strong liquor, the kind of booze that could substitute for paint thinner. No wonder he'd lost his shit and cuffed Ceres one, even if it didn't excuse his barbaric behavior in the slightest. The wolf in me also picked out the damning scent of a woman and sex all over him.

Craig barged in past me as if he owned the place, stumbling over the door's threshold.

"How'd you get here?" I closed the door and hoped the noise didn't wake Ceres.

"Walked. I crashed at the party a few blocks over... Where's my girl?"

"You sure you wanna talk to her like this, dude?" To top off the rest, he smelled like weed, as if he'd bathed in ganja all night long prior to guzzling a keg of beer all on his own. "You're fucking toasted."

"The fuck're you now, dude? Her dad? Where the fuck is she? Is that cunt upstairs?"

Cunt? Of all the things to call a woman, that wasn't a word I'd ever use. I saw red and fought to restrain myself. On any other day, I would have sent him packing out of my house with my fist. After my night, I lacked the patience to deal with his bullshit.

An impulsive answer parted from my lips, uttered without actual thought. "She's downstairs in the basement getting her luggage. She said something about going home for the rest of the weekend. She's only planning to come back for graduation, then she's gonna leave with her family again. You know Ceres. Daddy's girl."

"We were supposed to go back together to visit my parents in Houston. She leaving now?"

"Looks like it, man." My fake smile strained my face.

An idea flit through my mind. If I wanted Ceres, if I wanted to ever have a chance — Craig had to back the fuck off and respect my domain. Teaching him a lesson was the first step to enacting the most ridiculous plot I'd ever concocted in my life. I'd fuck him up so hard he wouldn't be able to tell the cops what happened once I finished.

"Basement's that way," I directed him patiently. We kept a lot of stuff in the lower level, including the gym equipment I'd gradually collected over the months. I clicked the light on at the top of the stairs then we descended into the dim chamber. He didn't even think to ask why the lights were off. Stupid bastard.

"Where the fuck is she?"

I didn't think. I struck violently at him with a fist to the back of the head. First, he screamed profanities at me then he stumbled forward into an inelegant sprawl face-down on the floor. Before he could get to his feet, I kicked him hard in the balls. And I kicked him again. I kicked him for Ceres and all the times he humiliated her in public. For all the times I heard him call her a vapid bitch. For all the times he left her high and dry while I had to give her a hand. At the end, I kicked him again for me: because he had the woman I wanted. The woman that should have been my mate. *Mine.*

"You motherfuck—FUCK!" he screamed when I kicked him a final time.

Down in this basement, no one could hear us. I'd drop his drunk ass out on the stoop and lock the door again once I finished. Craig was a big guy and my physical superior, but my sober mind and animal instincts had the advantage. In a fair fight, he would have pounded me into paste. I had no doubt that his pride would never allow him to fess up to the identity of his assailant.

But this wasn't a fair fight. This was stone cold vengeance, and I wasn't human.

"You fucking fag. When I get off this floor I'm gonna kill you!"

"When you get off the floor? You could barely walk down the fucking stairs."

Craig scrambled to his hands and knees, and then he lunged at me. I'd underestimated the pain-numbing effect of alcohol, and that was my downfall. The ground jumped up at me.

"Fucking pussy. I always knew you'd try some shit like this." He punched me once, his fist a sledgehammer to my face. I blocked the second, but he drove his knuckles into my body instead and crushed all the air out of my lungs. I couldn't breathe, but I recovered enough to tussle with him on the workout mat.

His meaty forearm laid across my windpipe and applied pressure to my throat. I couldn't breathe and the world around me lost focus.

I'm stronger than this. I'm stronger than this asshole.

I bashed my fist against his temple, but a tilt of his head rolled the punch off his brow without doing massive damage. Fear of suffocation kicked my fight or flight instinct into high gear.

No. Not now.

I fought it and resisted the call to transition to my wolf body. Jagged lances of pain struck me in my torso and twisted my limbs. *No!* My contorting body arched against the floor as a claw curved from each of my shortening fingers. The very moment he realized something was wrong, Craig's entire expression changed from gloating victory to terror. He staggered back in time to save his pretty face from my snapping jaws.

"Fuck no. No fucking way this is happening. Oh shit!"

It was too late to refuse the inner beast inside me. The wolf raged, a snarling monster that no longer resembled my human self. My hackles were up, my belly hungered for retribution, and nothing, no amount of screaming, would deny me what was mine.

***

I awakened an hour later on the bloodied workout mat, surrounded by the remnants of Ceres' boyfriend. Choking on the vile taste, I twisted over onto my side and stared into his dead eyes.

"No," I croaked out. I had a dead man in my basement. "Fuck!" My fingers shook as I ran them through my hair. Darting my gaze around, I tried to think what I needed to do. I had a dead man in my basement. I'd *killed* a human in my own domain, breaking one of the oldest laws. The first law Ceres ever taught me.

If I couldn't tell my pack and I couldn't tell the mortal police, what could I do? The answer came to me with sudden clarity. I phoned Harrison for help.

"Man, you didn't? Tell me you didn't lose your wolfy shit in your basement of all places." Harrison groaned. "Don't y'all have rules about that kind of thing?"

"Yeah, we do, but I need our help quick before... fuck. Sunrise is soon. I don't know what I'm doing. It's too much."

"Okay, okay. Do what you can until I get there with the kit. For fuck's sake, you know better than this." Harrison hung up on me and arrived in record time.

It took us most of the morning to bag Craig's corpse, the evidence, and scrub the basement. By the time I concluded my work, I was drenched in sweat, and my hair was plastered against my face. One shower wasn't enough. I left it feeling filthy and in need of several more.

Harrison shot me a dirty look every five minutes, but he had more experience in this kind of deal than I did. Raven shifters and werewolves had a centuries-long history, working alongside one another as comrades. When wolves like me fucked up, ravens like him made the mess disappear.

"Dad said you better hope nobody saw him coming this way. You'll have the police all up your ass."

"You told your dad?"

"Well, yeah. He asked why I was coming out with the kit. You're pretty lucky your grandparents' place has this little hideaway crawlspace beside the basement. Whenever I visit, I'll take a few more pieces of him with me."

"How long is it going to take?"

"A week tops. I promise you won't even know he's down here until then. Go shower again. I'll finish up here," Harrison said.

I'd barely shut the basement door behind me when Ceres stepped into view. My chest heaved with exertion. I must have looked like a crazed man to her, and if she thought that, she isn't too far from the mark. I'd killed a human, even if it was in self-defense, and I had no choice but to truck on and pray I didn't see his face in my nightmares.

An uncertain smile flitted across her features, and then her concerned green eyes traveled over my dirty sweats and sweat-stained tee. "Are you okay? What happened to your face?"

"Yeah. I'm cool. Nothing big. Harrison came over early to help with some plans I had for the basement. Men's work. Then I tripped over a barbell I left on the floor."

"Are you—?"

"Anyway, I'm gonna get a shower," I mumbled. I avoided eye contact to slip past her into the narrow hallway, eager to avoid more awkward questions. Part of me thought that if we locked gazes, she'd see the truth and know the reality of my crimes.

Or that she'd smell the blood.

"I made lunch—"

"Not hungry." I shut the bedroom door in her face and paced for a half hour, struggling to process the morning's events that had caught up to me.

"Tommy?" she called again through the door. "Are you—?"

"No, I'm not fine. Just leave me alone, okay?"

"Tommy... Is this about last night? Look, I'm sorry. Really, I am. Can we talk about it?"

"I'll be out in a few. Just getting some stuff together so I can shower. I'm sweaty and gross and I overdid it with the weights." Heaving around a dead football player was the ultimate workout apparently. I'd feel it by evening.

"Okay... I'll make you a plate," she spoke up hopefully.

About a half hour later, I left the bathroom and encountered a full-blown luncheon. When Ceres wanted to butter me up, she usually prepared a feast. Today was no exception.

"The hell is all this?"

A plate stacked tall with roast beef and horseradish cheddar sandwiches waited for me on the table next to a bowl of my favorite salsa and chips. That part was easy enough, sure. But she'd also made coleslaw and her mom's German potato salad. Sliced lemons floated in a pitcher of iced tea. My eyebrows rose toward the top of my skull when she pulled a tray of cookies from the oven. Was I in the shower long enough for this?

"A meal?" she replied. Her puzzled response sounded like a question to my ears. Like she didn't know what the hell she was doing either.

"You haven't gone into full Betty Crocker mode in months," I pointed out.

"Well... School is over now and I wanted to do something nice for you. So sit and eat already, okay?" She poured my drink and set it down in front of me.

"Did Harrison leave?" Part of me worried he'd emerge from the basement at any moment, covered in the blood of my enemy.

"Yeah, he shouted something about having a lunch date to get to. Left in a rush."

I stuffed my face to swallow the taste of her rejection... and Craig. Eventually, the awkward air between us cleared, allowing friendly conversation about the upcoming graduation. She looked forward to that, and truthfully, so did I.

"Hey, Tommy?"

"Yeah?" I reached for another cookie from the plate centered on the table.

"Thanks for being a good friend."

A boyfriend-killing friend, I thought, but wisely kept the remark to myself. I used her cookies as an excuse for silence.

"What for exactly?" I finally inquired after the third cookie. She refilled my glass of tea to the top and collected the plates littering the table.

"Cheering me up last night.

If I didn't see the evidence with my own eyes, I'd have never discovered Craig's abusive tendencies. Ceres had applied her makeup well. Aside from the slight puffiness bordering her lower eyelid, no other trace of the damage remained. That kind of work required both talent and practice, leaving me to wonder one thing: how many bruises had she hidden behind foundation and powder until her wolf healing smoothed it away? I'd never know.

The thoughts made me regret my actions a little less. I had even less remorse for the intimacy shared between us. If I had it to do again, I'd repeat my actions in a heartbeat.

"Beth's giving me a ride over to Craig's place so I can talk to him and break up. Don't wait up for me, all right?"

Good luck there. Butterflies of anticipation fluttered in my belly. I didn't want to face the consequences of my actions. I didn't even know if it was an accident now. Craig had it coming to him, and deep down, something in my subconscious rejoiced. The wolf in me celebrated his death and *my* victory.

Ceres dipped down to kiss my cheek in passing. Her lips left a warm feeling in their wake, joined by an indescribable longing for more. She mussed my hair, grabbed her purse from the chair, and left me with the dishes.

All the while I cleaned and restored the kitchen to its state prior to Hurricane Ceres, I anticipated the possible outcomes of Craig's disappearance. How long would it take the police to suspect foul play? Without a body, they couldn't prove anything.

Callers began to phone Ceres for Craig by the end of the day. When visiting his place didn't work, she tried to ring him again on his cell. Thankfully, I'd had Harrison and his expertise. After he disassembled Craig's phone, a couple ravens flew the pieces out over the gulf. Nobody would be tracking that baby with GPS or finding a piece of evidence in my basement.

By the second day, circulating gossip revealed he'd spent the night drinking, smoking pot, and getting head from a skanky girl at the party. No one saw him leave afterward, and no one knew where he'd gone. His bike remained on the road outside the farmhouse until a relative retrieved it Tuesday evening.

I was wrong to expect our friendship to return to its usual dynamic. Ceres distanced herself from me over the days since our near-tryst on the sofa. It all came to a head on the morning of her graduation, after her parents phoned and announced they would fetch us both.

We were rocking on the metal swinging bench beneath the covered porch when she turned to me.

"I wish I knew what happened to Craig," she murmured.

"You're still concerned about him? The asshole punched you in the face and spent the rest of his night getting his dick sucked."

"Don't you have any empathy for others, Tommy? Any at all? He's *missing*."

"Of course I care that he's missing, I just don't see why you're so worried."

She spent most of the day alternating between dirty looks and watching me through distrustful eyes. After the graduation ceremony, I approached her to congratulate her for a job well done, and she hugged me awkwardly as if I was the creepy uncle she feared touching with her tits.

Once the big event wound down, her father invited me to fill in Craig's spot in their dinner party. I tried politely to refuse and head home, but her mother insisted. No one says no to Vesta Prescott, our mother of the pack.

Ceres picked at her dinner and remained quiet. Her parents tried to lure her into conversation but her stony silence unnerved them until they interrogated me instead. I knew it was coming from the moment Ceres excused herself to the restroom to check her makeup. She was wise to conceal her bruised face. If I hadn't killed Craig, her father would have made my retribution look like child's play.

"Tell us what happened, Thomas," her mother said.

"I don't really know what to tell you," I said. I couldn't lie to Vesta; she knew me too well, a second mother to me after my own passed away. I decided to skirt the truth instead.

"I've never seen Ceres so upset. Not since she lost the chance to become Prom Queen," her father said, shaking his head.

"I know you, and I know when you're hiding something. What is going on with Craig and Ceres?" her mother insisted. Her worried gaze broke through my conscience.

"She and Craig had a fight. Now nobody knows where he's gone. That's really all I know."

"Such a shame you two—"

"Vesta," her husband interjected in a quiet, firm voice. Argus took care of his family with old money, his earnings as a lawyer, and successful investments. As the Alpha, he governed our supernatural lives, and I'd be lucky to leave town alive if they found out what I'd done.

"Oh, you know you've said the same. But fine. I just hope she'll get over it soon. He was too young for her anyway. And... human. She knows we won't approve of another bite."

"Sweetheart, you also know that Ceres is stubborn. She never goes for the guys you try to set her up with," Argus reminded her.

"She's a spoiled little bitch," Vesta snapped bluntly. Argus tried to remove the wine glass from Vesta's hands, but she curled her fingers tightly around the stem.

The topic of conversation made me want to squirm in my seat.

"You're quite the grown man now, Thomas. I'm so glad we voted in your favor."

"Now Vesta, let's not put Tommy on the spot."

"And handsome, too. Craig looks like a bulldog someone's molded into a man." She sniffed disdainfully. "He lacks your grace. Your finesse. Could you imagine him on a hunt?" she continued despite her husband's attempt to silence her.

Seriously, how long did it take for a woman to pee? I wanted Ceres to come back so the attention would shift away from me again.

Vesta sipped her wine while her husband looked on in defeated resignation. His role as our pack Alpha didn't give him control over his wife. Vesta always spoke her mind, and once she hit the bottle for a while, unfiltered honesty poured from her with impunity. "Don't you think he looked like a pug-nosed mutt, Thomas?" she asked me. Loudly.

"Er, well..."

"Oh, come on. Don't be shy," she encouraged me.

"Vesta—"

"Oh shut it, Argus. I'm only asking the man his opinion. There is nothing criminal about that. If you'd man up and stop allowing that spoiled little brat of yours to ruin her life, you'd give your opinion, too."

Several eyes turned our way, and I felt hot beneath my collar. The Prescotts argued in not so very hushed tones while I wished I had ordered that drink they offered. I took a long swallow from my soda instead.

Ceres' return heralded a swift change in topic, not that she contributed much to the conversation. Her mother baited her again and snapped unveiled insults about her career choice until I intervened by distracting her. After dinner, her parents dropped us off and Ceres headed inside ahead of me.

"Hey, Tommy?"

"Yes, sir?" I paused on the walkway and turned to face their parked car. It idled alongside the curb, engine running. Vesta dozed in the passenger seat.

"Ceres didn't stiff you on the bills again, did she?"

"What? N-no. She paid her share."

"Well, anyway, I'd still like to give you a little extra something for putting up with Vesta tonight," Argus said. He fished out his wallet and wrote a check.

As usual, I protested and held out both hands to ward off his money.

"You take this and unwind with it. You've got your usual trip to Las Vegas coming up soon, right?"

My pride and dignity resisted the check, but my ailing bank account salivated. I took it without reading the amount. Argus waved goodbye and pulled the black Tahoe away from the curb.

Once again hurt by her mother's callous behavior, Ceres spent the remaining hours sobbing in her bedroom upstairs. I ached for her too, but she didn't want my comfort or company. I let her alone to heal on her own terms.

CHAPTER 5

~THOMAS~

To be honest, I don't recall much of the six nights away in Vegas. It was a blur of gambling at the casino, drinking at the clubs, and tucking dollar bills in sweaty thongs at the strip clubs. My wallet was a lot lighter when I returned home, but I had a good time. We'd made the trip every year since college. Bros and hoes.

Harrison dropped me off, and I trudged inside, ready to sleep off a hangover. A plastic wrapped plate of my favorite turtle blondie brownies sat on my dresser with a crayon drawing of a dinosaur. The accompanying note from Jamie said he wanted to share his mom's desserts with me. I greedily devoured three before passing out fully dressed on my bed.

Sometime around noon the next day, I dragged myself from the bed and showered. Ceres ambled down to ask about my weekend but the stilted conversation between us sent her back up the stairs with a drink and chips.

I sighed. "Gonna go out and mow!" I called upstairs.

"Okay." Her voice barely carried down to me. I'd seen Ceres depressed before, but never like this, and I didn't want to push her into talking too soon.

I gave her space by going outside. In my baseball cap, t-shirt, and jeans, I hopped into the tractor and cruised it onto the grass. Texas sunshine is brutal but the wolf in me loved the outdoors. Inhaling the sweet scent of fresh clipped grass, I reveled in the cool breeze and took a break beneath my gran's ornamental shade trees. Sweat trickled down my back and soaked into my grey t-shirt until I removed it altogether. It took an hour to wrangle both my yard and Emma's.

"As much as I appreciate you doing this, you know you don't have to." Emma managed to surprise me since the grass and wind direction masked her scent. The lawn mower had muted her approach.

"I didn't realize you were home, Miss Ke— Emma. Where's your car?"

Hot damn, she was sexy today. A quick glance turned into a roving look. Emma wore her maroon tank top one size too tight, or maybe her tits were one size too large for the proportion to fit. Denim Capris hugged her hips and an ass I wanted to fuck. Her long hair was braided back and part of me wanted to find out how many times I could wrap it around my fist. My tenant was a petite, voluptuous package I couldn't look at without thinking inappropriate thoughts.

"It's in the shop for a brake replacement. I'm going to walk over and pick it up when Jamie gets home."

"Nah, don't do that. I can drive you two down there." It would be a miserable trek across town in this weather with the wind kicking up dust. Our town also lacked sidewalks on most streets.

"That's nice of you to offer, but I don't want to put you out. I, uh, actually came out here to bring you this. You look like you could use a cold drink." Emma offered me a glass of lemonade, which I chugged and handed back to her in seconds.

"Ready for that ride now?"

"On the tractor with a sweaty man?" Her impish grin led my thoughts right back into the gutter.

"Heh. Fair enough. I'll go get cleaned up then meet you out front."

Jamie was home by the time I doused myself in a shower and returned. I gave the pair a ride to fetch her car then we met at Dairy Queen for Blizzards.

Harrison was right. One afternoon outing away from home helped me realize that socializing with other people was exactly what I needed to bring me out of my funk. On the way home, I phoned him and the guys up to make plans for a night at the sports bar.

~CERES~

I needed to get out of the house, but all of my girlfriends were busy with other summer plans. If they weren't beginning their internships or working, they were away on family vacations or visiting distant places. Meanwhile, I sulked back home in Atropos and wished I'd taken Dad up on his offer to go to Disney. Pretending to be his little girl again would have beaten out sitting upstairs alone and wishing Thomas would fess up.

How long is he going to hide it and pretend Craig ran off on me?

After a shower, I tossed on a flirty, strapless sundress in a sunny yellow color. It fell to my thighs and bounced around my long legs. Worn with heels or wedges, I would be too tall, so I opted for ivory flip flops and knocked on Emma's door a few minutes later.

"Hi," I greeted when the door opened to frame Emma's petite body. She wore a black tank and green, fairy-themed pajama bottoms that had seen better days.

"Hello. Is something wrong?"

"Wrong? Oh, no! Tommy didn't send me for anything," I quickly explained. "I know we haven't talked much, but I noticed, um… well your little boy was very polite when he brought those brownies over for Thomas. I kind of snuck one, too."

"Really?" A big smile lit over her face as she opened the screen door. "Would you like to come in? I have more."

"Actually… I noticed Jamie goes down to the Boys & Girls Club during the week and you're usually gone to work by now, but since you're home… would you like to do something?" She seemed the homebody type, always single and rarely leaving the house in anything but her work clothes.

Emma blinked at me. "Like what?"

"There's Mabel's cafe for lunch, and Katie Parrish opened a new thrift store in the middle of town. It's called Girls+ and has, um, sizes from me to you."

She twisted to glance behind her at the clock on the wall. It revealed the time was almost lunch hour, perfect for hitting the small strip of family-owned businesses in our town.

"Not a bad idea. Thrift store goods are about all I can afford until I get a better job," she confessed.

I sat in the living room for a while as Emma prepared for the day. She met me in denim Capris and a Star Wars t-shirt. We bonded over a mutual love for Vader during the walk, grateful for the overcast day that didn't assault us with a sweltering Texas sun.

"Lunch first?" she asked when the sidewalk from our neighborhood merged with Main Street. Another half mile south would bring us down a strip of family owned shops and the local town grocery.

"I dunno…" I peeked at the watch charm dangling from my bracelet. "Are we going to fit into as many awesome secondhand things if we're bloated from eating greasy diner cuisine?"

"Point."

The cramped consignment shop held a larger selection than anticipated, hiding rare gems on the organized racks and display tables. I plucked up several items and passed them over for Emma to try on.

"This one has a plunging neckline I'd never be able to pull off."

I stared at her. "What are tits that big good for if you're not going to show them?" I demanded.

She bought the dress and I picked up a new pair of cutoffs for a dollar. A couple bucks later, we vacated the shop and continued down the lane, chatting animatedly about our lack of places to wear our new things.

Emma and I settled at the tiny cafe table and peered at the paper menus. The waitress brought us tall glasses of sweet tea. After we placed our orders, we settled into a conversation that led to me sharing things I'd never told another person.

"I'm feeling incredibly popular lately. Yesterday Tommy took Jamie and me to Dairy Queen, now I'm having lunch with you. Why doesn't Tommy ever take *you* anywhere?"

"Like where?" I asked, bewildered.

"You know, dates. It's not like you have kids holding you up at—"

"Whoa, whoa, whoa. Back up. Tommy isn't my boyfriend."

Something about Emma made me bare my soul. I told her everything, excluding our true natures and the make out on the sofa. "So that's us in a nutshell. He asked a few times back in high school, but I never let it go anywhere. When Mom really started to hammer me about not being like her and going to medical school, I needed an escape."

"So Tommy let you move in with him."

"Yeah. It was Dad's idea. He put me up to asking and said he'd give me enough cash to help Tommy with the bills while I'm here."

The waitress reappeared with our orders and set both plates in front of us. We'd both ordered overstuffed sandwiches filled with shaved meat, cheese, and bacon. A dill pickle spear and mountain of sweet potato fries flanked each sandwich.

"I honestly can't believe the two of you aren't together," Emma admitted once the server left.

I chuckled and shook my head. "It's not like we're the first man and woman living in the same house as friends."

"Yeah, but you're both hot, so people's minds want to jump to the other conclusion." Emma shrugged her shoulders and nibbled a fry. I eyed the neglected pickle on her plate. Mine was already gone.

"You gonna eat that?" She shook her head and offered it to me. Tommy never wanted his pickles either.

"My parents want us together, but to be really honest with you, I was always afraid it would ruin what we had."

Emma's sympathetic nod endeared her to me even more. I liked her open and honest personality. "That's always a good reason not to take things to the next level. Friendship matters more than sex."

"Right," I agreed. "I'm so glad to talk to you about this. None of my friends really understand."

"Why's that?"

"They all think I should just jump his bones and get it out of my system. Or his."

Emma shook her head. "That's not the way to do things. He's hot as hell, but leaping into bed with him isn't going to fix everything."

"He really is hot," I agreed with a sigh. "So now you know why I live in this town away from home. What about you? Do your parents live nearby?"

"Oh no," Emma said quickly, shaking her head. "They're in Wisconsin. I uh…" She sucked in a breath then released it in a laugh, color seeping into her cheeks. Her warm, brown skin tone was beautiful. "I met this boy one day from Texas. I was stupid, got pregnant, and let him convince me to move here to

Texas. My parents hated the idea, but they didn't fight it because my Aunt Nina lives close by."

"So what happened to the guy? I mean, if you don't mind telling me."

"He got picked up by a basketball scout about a month later. Decided a baby and I didn't fit into his NBA life."

"Yeah?" I turned to her with interest. "Which player? Which team?"

"Doesn't matter now. He's in prison for underage sex charges."

I winced. "Karma?"

"I like to think so. Anyway, I was too ashamed to go back home to the reservation, and Aunt Nina took me in. Jamie sees my mother and father when I can afford our flight up north, and his other grandparents… I send him for a week or two over the summer. They're nice people."

"It isn't their fault that their son's a dick."

"Yep," she agreed. "It's nice they want to be involved with Jaime and it gives me time to unwind by myself."

Being around Emma muddied up my feelings for Thomas. One moment, he was all I had in my thoughts, an all-consuming presence that constantly made me think about his smiles, or how electrifying it felt when I passed him a cup of coffee in the morning and our fingers had touched. In the next moment, Emma became my top priority.

And by the end of the meal, I felt like a fool for waiting so long to get to know her. "We need to leave Jamie with Tommy and take off somewhere together."

"Like where?" Emma asked.

"A movie, hell, a club somewhere in San Antonio. Anywhere."

The waitress came with our bill, and before Emma could reach for her wallet, I slipped three tens on the check and sent the server away.

"Thanks for hanging out with me today, Emma. Thank you. I just…" Hardly wanting to become emotional in public, I struggled to stave off the burning tears blurring my vision. "I really needed someone today."

"Sweetie, it's nothing. Any time you need to talk, and you see my car out there, you're free to come over."

"Thanks."

I held the door open for her as we made our way outside onto the sidewalk. The skies had darkened, rolling in ominous clouds of gray. A distant rumble thundered across the heavens as hot wind tousled our hair. We were subjected to an oppressive blanket, its weight urging us home at a brisk pace, until the first showers began. Then we ran, giggling the entire while as we sprinted up the path to my house and burst onto the covered porch.

Tommy's truck wasn't in the drive. I sent him a quick text and received an equally curt response.

"Tommy went out for beer, so I guess we're all alone… Wanna come on inside?"

To my great fortune, Emma made amazing mixed drinks. While Tommy fetched his beer from the liquor store, she and I got into his booze collection and helped ourselves to his stash of hard liquor and sweet-flavored cordials.

"Is he going to mind?"

"No, he'll take it as an excuse to buy more. He's always bringing home *something*."

With our iced drinks in hand, we got comfy on the couch while the flickering lights heralded a possible outage.

"Hey, Emma? I need some advice."

"Shoot."

"What would you do if someone close to you told you a lie, but you already knew it?"

"People lie for different reasons, Ceres. I guess it depends on why they're being dishonest, and whether I'm willing to give them the chance to come clean."

"So you think lying can be okay in certain circumstances."

"It's a fine line, Ceres. I mean, we all tell little white lies, right? And sometimes we lie to protect people. But too many falsehoods just lead down a slippery slope." Emma set her hand against my arm with a light touch. "Why?"

"Uh… a guy I sort of like… well, no. I'm crazy about this guy and wanted to ask him out — well, he fibbed to me about something."

"So Tommy lied to you about something?"

I sighed. "Busted."

"You were about as subtle as a hammer to the skull. Obviously you're into him now, and he's not dating anyone so maybe you should just ask him out," she suggested.

"I always thought you had a bit of a crush on him, actually. You bring him all sorts of sweets."

"I bring sweets for *both* of you," she corrected, her tone patient. But she didn't quite meet my eyes either. "Because you're awesome neighbors and he's a great landlord. He's just… out of my league."

Before I could interrogate Emma, Tommy's truck made its noisy return. I canted my head and listened for his steps on the porch then the door opened. The rain made his t-shirt cling against his torso, cotton sticking to hard muscles and a lean physique I'd often fantasized about in my dreams.

"Hi, Emma." Tommy's blue eyes wandered to me last. "Gonna go work in the basement."

He thundered down the stairs and shut the door behind him.

"That's one step above the silent treatment, right?"

"Do you think I should bring him a drink?" Emma was still staring at the closed door, brows furrowed. "How long have you two been this, uh, tense?"

"Since a few days before he went away on his usual trip." I struggled to maintain a level voice without tears streaming down my face.

"Why don't you go put your new duds away and I'll see what I can do."

CHAPTER 6

~THOMAS~

I knew it was Emma at the door before she opened it to come downstairs. I'd set my case of beer aside on the table and cranked up the music, prepared for an hour of extensive working out. As she descended the stairs with a margarita in her hand, fresh rain, salt, and the stronger, natural aroma of her flesh called to me.

Emma whistled as my assault on the heavy bag continued. I had long ago discovered that exercise was the best outlet for my aggression. The wolf in me demanded three things — food, violence, and sex — and not always in that order. Emma couldn't provide any of those things, nor could I live with myself if I hurt her. So I focused. I channeled my anger and my lust into my fists until my bare knuckles were raw.

"Tommy?"

I caught the bag and stilled it, then dropped both arms down to my sides before I turned to face her. "What's up?"

"We thought you'd like to maybe join us for a drink." Ice clinked in the glass she offered out in temptation. The lime and tequila had nothing on the brown sugar scent clinging to her tawny skin. "But since you seem distracted, I thought I'd bring the drink to you."

Shallow breaths through my nose didn't help when her essence had already wrapped around me, wafted by the fan blowing on high. I closed my eyes, bid my wolf to remain calm, and maintained my cool. I opened my eyes to find her studying me closely. Most humans would have sensed something was off and fled by now, unless they were like Craig and too dumb to feel the danger. Emma didn't strike me as dumb, so I wondered why she stuck around with a smile.

"Thanks." I took a sip right off, letting the strong drink distract me from how badly I wanted to fill Emma with my dick.

"Is everything okay? You bee-lined down here pretty fast."

"Yeah, I'm good. Didn't wanna intrude on girl time." *Since when did the two of them begin to hang out?*

"You aren't, but if you change your mind you're welcome to join us." She hesitated at the foot of the stairs and glanced back at me when I returned to my boxer's stance. "You're pretty good at that. Did you take lessons?"

"Not really. Ceres' dad and her godfather taught me back when I was in high school. I had... anger issues." Problems with controlling my wolf. As a way to vent my aggression, Argus introduced me to boxing and taught me everything he knew. I really learned how to fight when her godfather Ian came to town on leave from the military. "Want a lesson?"

"Sure."

I blinked.

"Thought I'd say no?" she teased.

"Well, yeah. All right, get over here then."

Ceres didn't like to spar bare hands like me, so I fetched her wraps and had Emma extend both arms toward me. With tender care, I wrapped each finger and protected her knuckles. Passing in front of the fan to approach the heavy bag wafted her scent toward me again, an irresistible tease to my animal senses.

"Did you just growl at me?"

"What? No," I denied quickly.

"I can leave if you want to be alone, Tommy."

"I was clearing my throat," I lied.

She didn't look convinced but she didn't mention it again. "So, is this how I stand?" Emma asked, imitating what I'd been doing.

"Tuck your elbows in a little more. You're not a chicken," I teased. A light-hearted laugh with Emma cooled me down from the edge. Together, she and Ceres had been impossible to resist, but alone, I managed to fight off the animal attraction. "There, that's better."

She adjusted her stance with minimal direction, like a natural taking the stage. A few hits later and I knew something was up. She had great form, and when I held the bag to prevent it from swinging about wildly, she struck it hard enough to move me, too.

"You're a little too good at this," I commented once beads of perspiration dotted her brows.

"I had lessons at the gym a few years back," she admitted. "But I couldn't afford to keep them up."

"You were humoring me all this time?"

"You seemed like you needed it."

Emma stripped the hand wraps and rolled them back up, flashing me a cherubic smile. Her dimpled cheek soothed any insult I felt at the deception. She left me in better spirits once she returned to Ceres upstairs, but I remained downstairs to resume putting my body through the ringer.

All of my discomfort didn't begin to fade until hours after Emma left our house. Even then, I had Ceres to contend with. I showered, fetched a couple shopping bags from the truck, then went upstairs to retrieve her.

"Hey." I poked my head in her open room after knocking on the doorframe. "There's something I wanna show you."

"Can it wait? I just wanna go to bed. I had a loooong afternoon shopping with Emma in town."

The skimpy pajama set revealed enough of her ass cheeks to make her bedtime plans apparent. I glanced over her and suppressed the thrill induced by her choice of clothing. Pink had never looked better on anyone.

"C'mon, Ceres," I persisted. Something told me to change my approach, instinct, or maybe frustration. "I have a surprise for you, and I want to give it to you. *Now.*"

Interest sparked in her eyes, attributed to either the word 'surprise' or my tone. I never took that kind of voice with her. "Okay!"

Ceres followed me into the kitchen where I'd set up my insulting array of gifts. She looked at them without realizing they were intended for her.

"Okay, Tommy. Where's my surprise?"

"Right there."

Initially, her big smile remained frozen in place. It cracked and faded seconds later. "What the hell's all this?"

The back corner of the kitchen held a dog bed, water bowl, and dish of canned dog. With Ceres distracted by the objectionable present, I fished the dog collar from my pocket and whipped it around her throat. A push of my thumb clicked the lock into place. Being a werewolf male meant I was physically stronger, but that didn't stop Ceres from fighting like a hellcat. Her nails gouged into my wrists and clawed my arms. She screamed, twisted, and elbowed me, but she never took her wolf form. If she had, I would have had a problem. She was faster than me *and* the better fighter.

"Tommy? What the fuck?" she demanded. When scratching and kicking at me didn't work, she struggled against the collar with both hands, hooking her fingers into it.

"I figured since you like it when guys treat you like a dog, maybe that's where I went wrong."

When my snide attitude and harsh words didn't provoke her into shifting for a fight, the crazy plan continued. It was too late to back down and risk looking like a fool. She'd never respect me again.

Ceres had another plan in mind. She tackled me to the tile floor. She scratched, clawed, and bit at me, as wild in a human body as she would be in a wolf form.

"Ceres!"

"Get this off of me!"

We tussled on the floor until I regained the upper hand during our struggle. We were both hot and sweating by the time I pinned her arms. While resisting the urge to lick my wounds, I watched her struggle and rehearsed my confession. I had to tell her about Craig, the way she made me feel, and the way it hurt to watch her make one poor choice after the next.

"I thought you liked it when a guy slapped you around and mistreated you. What's different now," I taunted her.

Ceres glared daggers at me, choosing to exercise her defiance through silence.

"We need to talk about a lot of things going on in this house. The way you treat me and the way you treat yourself."

She didn't answer me.

"Don't you get sick of it? Don't you get tired of no-good lowlifes like Craig treating you like shit when you deserve better? You're not a dog, Ceres, but when I look at the way your boyfriends treat you in your relationships, this is how I see you." Her cool stare unnerved me.

"Craig would have never put a dog collar on me."

"Yeah, he only embarrassed you in front of his friends and laid you out during a party. Craig's gone now, Ceres." I released her and let her off the floor.

"So you keep saying," she snapped.

My eyes narrowed and my jaw clenched. "I killed him. He showed up here the morning after he knocked you around, and I killed him. And I don't regret it. I *don't*. I lost my cool when dealing with him and had to call in Harrison to clean up my mess."

"You did that on your own?"

"What the hell else was I supposed to do? Leave him to rot? Explain a mangled body to the police? Call your dad and get kicked out of the pack?" The pack was family to me now, and hell if I planned to get tossed out because of one indiscretion. Most wolves had a mortal death or two on their hands, but the supreme difference was in the way it happened. The intent. I let a human provoke me into my wolf form and I murdered him by accident. That was my crime. Not that I'd done it at all, but that my rage got the best of me.

Ceres kicked at me as an answer.

"I'm tired of the cock teasing bullshit. If you don't want sex with me, if you don't want a relationship with me, fine. That's cool. But you keep taking this beyond flirting." I stepped closer and dared her to take another strike at me. She didn't. Her chin raised and her bright green eyes held my gaze. "You prance in front of me wearing everything from your closet that isn't a thong. All these years, the only thing you haven't done is lift your tail for me."

My dick twitched in my sweats, too hard to escape her notice. Ceres directed her gaze down to the apparent bulge at the front of the gray cotton then raised her eyes to my face again. "I never meant to hurt you, Tommy, not once, but you may as well let me go. I won't tell Dad you put a dog collar on me."

Our stare down continued. "Are you going to tell him I killed Craig?"

"No."

"Why not?"

"Is this really how you see me?" She gestured to the dog bowl.

"Yeah." I dragged in a breath. "And it hurts. It hurts me every time one of these guys breaks your spirit. Craig was the one I couldn't ignore."

Some sick part of me liked the looks of her with the collar on, its leather and steel attractive against her fair skin. My hard cock flexed again, but this time her fingers sought me and wandered over the unyielding bulge. With one forward step, my hips moved into the pressure of her hand. "Take my cock out. Touch it, Ceres. Touch *me*."

My heart hammered in my chest, the rush of blood filling my ears. Her quick breaths, the slight part to her thighs, and the way her tongue moistened her lower lip told me she was turned on. I smelled the damp cotton between her legs and the scent of her arousal permeating my senses, driving me like an unspoken command. Her body language said everything she wouldn't speak aloud.

"Touch me instead," she whispered.

I ripped her shorts down her thighs in one tug, revealing her sleek mound and bare hips. She didn't wear panties. I'd always suspected she didn't wear them under those tiny shorts. No longer able to deny the beast inside me, I gave in to my wolf. Ceres was mine, and I had to prove it.

I popped the thin spaghetti strap of her camisole and bared one small breast to my rough handling. I squeezed, kneading her tit in my hand, and even pinching her nipple while she surrendered her control. Her head fell back and her lips parted in a soundless sigh as my teeth scraped over the rosy tip.

Dragging her down to the floor was easy. All it took was a firm grip in her hair and my teeth at her throat then I positioned her on all fours. I nipped the sensitive skin behind her ear as I spread her thighs apart with the firm press of my knee between them, all the while waiting for rejection. She could have said no at any time and ended it right there, but as I bent my head down to inhale her lust, my tongue flickered against her slit and tasted the wet sheen glistening on her folds.

"I'm going to fuck you all night, you little bitch. You're mine."

"Thomas…"

Each tongue stroke was a promise of what was to come, a raw need overtaking all thought and reason until only the burning desire remained.

"Tell me you want it."

When she didn't answer, replacing my tongue with one finger made her shudder in place. She rocked forward and back, inviting me to penetrate her hole. I denied her.

"Tell me what you want or I walk away right now and this chance doesn't come again."

"No, don't!"

"Then say it," I commanded.

She trembled beneath me, fighting against her needs and her desires. "Fuck me if you have the balls to do it right, Tommy."

Her words had the intended effect — I wanted to cripple her and give her the most earth-shattering orgasm she'd ever experience in all of her life. I wanted to show her who was boss and service her, teach her a lesson and reward her. All of these things boiled together to the surface, conflicting and rolling together as one.

I pumped forward and claimed her in two hard strokes, spearing her tight entrance until our bodies clapped together. Her channel gripped me snug, wetter than I anticipated, a sure sign she'd desired me as much as I craved her. We both needed this.

Pistoning strokes claimed her with sensual tempo, driven by the urgency to outperform the memories of Craig. I didn't want her to even remember his name let alone recall how his cock felt inside her.

"T-Thomas, don't stop. Don't stop yet, baby, please," she pleaded.

"I won't." I'd promised her all night, and I meant to keep my word. Each thrust better than the last. I drove home to her full depth, grinded, and reached beneath her body to grope one tit. She groaned and fell onto her elbow when my balls bounced off her clit. The repetitive motion continued as our sex became a marathon, repeated each time I thrust to completion in her tight depths. Her body's core, slick with her arousal, greeted me like we were long lost friends finally reunited. This was where I belonged. Me and her, together at last.

How could one woman feel so great, so absolutely meant for me? My head tilted back in a silent, euphoric cry as her undulating hips met me stroke for stroke. She became more than a passive partner, but a lover, turning her head and groping until she seized a handful of my hair. Intuition made me follow her guidance and meet her lips in a tender kiss. Sweet, frenzied, and then finally desperate.

"Almost... So close. Ngh... right there, Thomas, right there!" When it came to Ceres, I couldn't settle for subpar sex. I had to prove I was worth her effort, worth the price of her submission, and that she'd never live to regret bending over for me on the cold floor.

A few times, she panted and moaned soft, appreciative sounds, almost too quiet for me to hear. Then she jerked beneath me and threw back her head, crying out a warning of her elation when I found her clit with my fingers. Her ecstasy was heard on every word of her triumphant shout. Pumping uneven strokes at varying depth, I finally felt the trembling spasm I needed. Her pussy clenched around me, one contraction after the next tightening her inner muscles until I was barely able to churn through her hot grasp. With a fistful of her hair in one hand, my hips surged forward and my balls tensed, heralding the spurt of cum that arrived with my claiming.

"*Mine,*" I snarled, too lost in the moment to stop.

Our moment lasted on and on, both of us moving, determined to extend our satisfaction. We fucked each other with frenetic rhythm until the last squeezes ended and we sank together to the kitchen floor. Spent, panting, and gleaming with sweat, I spooned my best friend and held her close. Giving her my cum had fulfilled the most basic condition of bonding. She was mine and I felt it through my soul.

I kissed her ear and set my cheek against her hair. Making love to Ceres was a head rush no amount of drugs, alcohol, or any other physical pleasure could ever hope to surpass. For a while, we were both content.

"We bonded," Ceres murmured.

"Yeah…" It felt so undeniably good to fulfill my wolf's urges after so long. It was like a cold drink of water on a hot July day, the most satisfying pleasure after an eternity of suffering. We lay like that for a while longer, nuzzling each other and exchanging brief kisses, the lull granting us the peace to recover from our wild union.

Ceres' whisper shattered the moment. "I don't know if we did the right thing."

I sat up and gazed down at her. "You can take a man who slaps you around and gets his cock sucked by some redneck bimbo in a barn, but you don't want to be bonded to me? Are you scared?"

She pushed up on one elbow and shook her head. "I'm not scared, Tommy. That's *your* issue. A single good fuck doesn't mean we're right for each other." Her lower lip trembled then she turned her head, wiping her cheek with the back of her hand. "A great fuck."

The sudden emergence of her tears took the wind from my sails and dulled my anger. "Why are you crying, Ceres? What's going on here?"

"How can I be bonded to a man who won't be honest with me? You lied to me all that time about Craig. I heard it. I smelled his blood, and I waited all this time for you to fess up to me."

A cold sensation swept over me, like a crashing wave at the beach. I stared at Ceres and opened my mouth soundlessly, closing again when no words came.

"You look like a fish," she whispered.

The insult spurred me out of my stunned silence. "You fucking knew all this time and never said anything?"

"He hit me. If you hadn't done something, I'd have given you up as a lost cause."

"I wanted to go and find him when I saw your face, Ceres. You don't know how much that pissed me off." If she knew about the killing, she probably knew all about my bad dreams since then, too. They plagued me often after killing Craig, and no matter how necessary it had been, how spontaneous the change came, I felt to blame for it.

She stepped forward to touch her index finger to my lips. "Shh… Obviously, I do since he's dead now. I'm not mad. I was never upset about Craig. Not even at my graduation. I was upset you didn't *tell me*."

"That's what the silent treatment was for?"

"I was hurt that you *lied* to me and couldn't step up to admit what you did!"

"Ceres…" I shoved both hands through my damp hair. "I broke the law, and your dad is the Alpha. I didn't want to drag you into it."

"That's a stupid excuse and you know it."

"So now what? What the fuck do we do now?" My fingers closed around her upper arm and pulled her to me. Kissing Ceres, my new mate, became the next priority on my mind. I enjoyed every second, savoring her sweet mouth and the way her hand slid from my nape into my hair. Her small tits pressed against my chest and the stiff nipples tickled my skin.

"I don't want this to end. I chased you all this time, and I'm not letting you go."

"Then don't." Ceres dragged in a shuddering breath and tilted her face up to mine. "For the first time in your life, Thomas, fight for what you want. Show me it's about more than this stupid bond." Her misty green eyes peered up at me, close to overflowing with tears. "Show me you love me with or without our wolves."

CHAPTER 7

~THOMAS~

Two deputies, one thin and the other too enormous to fit comfortably in a cruiser, showed up to talk to Ceres the next day. When I told them she wasn't in, they asked to discuss Craig's disappearance with me instead. I wiped my sweaty palms against my jeans and invited them into the foyer. I'd known these guys for a while. In fact, I'd fixed Deputy Richards' computer for his wife once and charged them a twenty to scrub the malware from it. She'd called me a good kid. Served me pecan pie and iced tea.

"You seem a little nervous, Mr. Weston," the balding cop said. The prominent nametag said his name was Mitchell, and while I didn't know him well, I recognized his face from escorting my grandmother to bingo nights at the VFW a few years back. She never missed a Thursday and neither did he.

"I was busy with something before you showed up."

He glanced at Granny's childhood photos of me decorating the foyer, most depicting me in all my chunky glory. A skeptical glance crawled over my muscled physique. "That you, son?"

"Yes, sir. I gave up pecan pie and fried chicken for a while. Granny was crushed." In a small town, it didn't benefit someone like me to be rude to the cops. Telling them to buzz off or come back made me look guilty, so I flashed a smile instead. "Y'all want some sweet tea or something? What can I do for you?"

Prior to their arrival, I'd been going over the basement floors with another layer of sealant. Harrison gave his word that there wasn't a shred of DNA left in the room, but he'd also suggested for us to paint and seal the floors. He never left anything to chance when on a job.

I really needed to talk to him one day about how often the ravens did that kind of body disposal work for other shifters.

"We'll try not to take up much of your time, Mr. Weston. Have you noticed any strange behavior between Ms. Prescott and Mr. Grey?" Deputy Mitchell asked.

"Nothing more than her usual behavior," I replied. I didn't have to lie. Ceres was a wild card, the sort of girl who could smile sweetly one second and flip a table the next. I blamed Vesta's head games and never held it against her, with exception of our big talk. "It's been a rough couple of weeks for Ceres. I guess she's kind of on a split from her boyfriend, and then she argued with her mother again over dinner a couple weeks week ago. It was pretty bad," I understated. Vesta was downright vicious. She never missed a chance to sock it to her daughter.

The men glanced at one another, communicating in nonverbal cop language. Deputy Richards, the taller one with graying hair, smiled at me and chuckled. "Normal for her age, I suppose. And what are you to Miss Prescott?" he asked.

I felt like a character in a crime drama. Confronted by the stereotypical fat cop and his handsome partner, I had no choice but to put on my best performance. "We're really good friends."

"Seems like you keep real busy around here. What about your mother and father?" Deputy Mitchell asked. His watery brown eyes scrutinized me.

"My father died while in the Service when I was a kid, and I don't remember much about him. And Mom died in a car wreck a year after I moved here for school."

"Sorry," Mitchell replied, abashed. My somber history received that reaction from most people. Everyone in town knew my grandparents were gone, but I never talked about my mother and father.

I forced a wan smile. Without waiting for the next question, I supplied what I suspected both cops wanted to know. "Craig came and beat on my door, I told him she was asleep, and he left. I haven't seen him since then."

Once I satisfied their queries, and the cops left my home, I sent a text message to Ceres. She didn't respond right away, but I expected that since she was at the movies. She returned home about an hour after I finished my work in the basement, hauling a heavy plastic sack with her. She'd brought take out, and it was stuffed.

"Mom and Dad gave me some money as a graduation gift. I don't have to mooch off of you so much this summer after all." They had also returned her car, much to my infinite relief. No more playing chauffeur for her and blowing through my gas.

"Yeah?" Between her promise to mooch less and the steaming hot smell of queso, she had my full attention. "Fuck yes, I smell my favorite."

"Carne asada burritos with extra guacamole on the side. I remembered."

"Thought you were gonna eat out with the girls?"

"I was going to, but then I remembered you were here and…" She had both hands behind her back, the toes of her left foot pointed toward the floor. She shyly glanced down at the tile. "I wanted to have dinner with you."

As Ceres set unpacked our dinner onto the coffee table, I fetched the bottle of tequila, sliced some lime wedges, and brought a couple glasses to join her at the sofa.

"Not too much, tonight. Dad called a pack meeting."

"When was I going to get a call about that?"

She laughed and pecked my cheek. "I said I'd pass it along. We live in the same house, silly."

It stung until she explained it that way. "You're right. Fine, two drink limit," I promised. Mexican just wasn't the same without the salty, punishing bite of a good tequila shot. Besides, I needed the drink for my nerves if I was going to face her dad down a second time without fessing up to my crime. Especially with her mating scent on my skin. Now that we were bonded, everyone would know.

Ceres fed me a few morsels from her plate, and I returned the favor until her lips closed over my index finger. Her suggestive look confirmed we shared mutual ideas and tempted me to ditch the food to skip straight to dessert. God, it was tempting, a better idea than attending our pack meeting for sure.

"We'll be late," I told her instead, pulling my hand back.

"Shit! You're right. I told Dad I'd show up early, too." Ceres caught my face between both hands and kissed me. "I'll meet you there. I wanna stop and do something along the way."

"Huh?"

"I said I'll take my own car and meet you out there, Tommy. Don't be late."

I sighed. Mate or not, some things didn't change. Once she was gone, I stored our leftovers in the fridge. The clock told me I had time, but any more delays would cut it close. Argus hated latecomers and made an example of them so I grabbed my keys and headed out.

"Hey, Tommy."

Jamie ran over with a football in his hands

"Sup, kid. How's it going?"

"I was trying to practice my throw but Michael said I suck. He called me wheezy." He kicked a rock off my driveway into the grass. His tight brown curls resisted my attempt to muss them, but the effort was worth the reward of seeing a smile on his face.

"Yeah, well, he's just jealous of how fast you can run kiddo."

"Do you wanna play with me?"

I glanced at my watch. "Ah crap... I have a meeting to get to, Jamie. Why don't you come over tomorrow and we'll work on your throwing arm, okay?"

"Okay. Thanks, Tommy."

He headed back across the grassy stretch between our houses and I hopped into my truck. Pack meeting grounds were on Argus and Vesta's property about a half hour from the San Antonio city limits. They owned an assload of acreage behind a massive fence, accessible only after entering a passcode at the gate located off the interstate. I pulled up to it after my drive and punched in the six-digit code.

Werewolves valued privacy and most of our kind had a large house on a lot of property. A lot. Deer, wild hogs, and sometimes the occasional cougar ran wild, but Argus had a taste for exotic animals and often bought some to let loose on their land. I hoped he bought another antelope soon.

I drove down a half-mile drive and parked in front of their triple story southern manor, the eighth vehicle in line on the horseshoe drive. Ceres was two cars ahead of me, which meant she'd already exposed everyone to our new scent.

"Cutting it close, aren't you, Weston?"

Jason Kennedy was everything I could never be. By that, I mean he's a jackass and nobody should *want* to emulate him. Guys like him gave alphas a bad name, and it bothered me that he was probably going to take over the pack one day or form his own. Because he was a strong wolf and favored by the older shifters like Vesta, the others ignored his indiscretions and let him treat them like shit.

"I'm five minutes early," I replied.

"Last one here. You know the drill, asshole. Think you'd get some extra privileges now or something?"

It was a damned shame nobody would let me punch the smug grin right off his square-jawed face. As the last arrival, I had the illustrious honor of serving the drinks and carrying the snack food platter around to our fellow wolves. It was a bitch job intended for omegas but given to the rest of us as punishment. I grinned through it and put on my smile, especially when Hector nudged me with a sly grin and nodded toward Ceres.

"About time," he said.

"Tell me about it."

About thirty-three adults and five cubs numbered our pack these days. Four of the cubs were born to parents new to our pack, transfers from the mid-west who wanted to begin anew in Texas. As for the fifth child, Argus had granted one-time breeding privilege to one of the older couples, Daphne and Hector. Procreation was treated as a serious matter among our kind because when shifters became too abundant, we choked an area and risked discovery. Only the best hunters and most loyal pack members were allowed a child.

"Let's begin." Any time Argus took the floor, every member of our pack went silent. No one had the audacity to disrespect the Alpha by giving him less than their full attention. "Our numbers have doubled in this decade. This pack is stronger than ever, and I owe our success to each of you for living by our rules. However, I can no longer govern a pack of this size."

He's going to step down. Fuck. It's true. Deep down, part of me had always known it was coming from his hints.

"And so the time has come to divide our numbers and choose another Alpha to lead our sister pack." All eyes turned toward Jason. He was on the edge of his seat, ready to rise and accept his victory. "While this role comes with many benefits, the responsibilities often outweigh the perks. I guide you, protect you, and I keep you safe from the predators of our world."

I shuddered. I'd heard stories of dragons who liked to buy shifters as slaves on the black market. We counted ourselves lucky that the powerful wyrms didn't keep any hoards in Texas. At least three dwelled in the mountains of California, and Argus told us one of the giant lizards, before her untimely death by sword, had collected animal shifters like stamps. Treated them like playthings. Fuck that. I didn't enter this life to become a pet.

"As the Alpha, you are more than a dictator. Every move and every decision affects countless lives. You'll have to know to do what's right, what's just, and what's the most efficient course of action to get the job done. It takes intellect and intuition. Your judgment may cost lives as well as save them."

Vesta cleared her throat. "Under normal circumstances, Argus and I would appoint a counterpart directly, but we have come to…" Her eyes drifted to her husband and lingered on his face. He smirked. "An impasse."

"At this time, I would appreciate any nominations for this role," the Alpha cut in.

"Jason," Vesta said. A few members voiced their approval and echoed the sentiment.

"Do you accept?" Argus asked.

"I do, sir," Jason said.

"I nominate Thomas," Ceres called to her father.

A startled expression surfaced on Vesta's face while her husband displayed a pleased smile. "Excellent choice, sweetheart. I second your nomination."

Vesta's face contorted, an ugly grimace adding years to her features and worsening her crow's feet. I choked on my drink until Daphne patted me on the back. Our Alpha Mother ran hot and cold with me like she needed a dose of lithium. Apparently she approved of me as a possible mate for her daughter, but disdained the thought of me leading a pack.

"I also agree with that nomination," her husband Hector said. "Thomas is a cunning hunter. He would make a great Alpha one day."

"One day," Jason argued. "Argus is talking about now."

"Good men become *great* men quickly when under duress. I believe in Thomas." Hector's big grin never faltered despite Jason giving him the stink eye.

If Daphne, Hector, Ceres, and even Argus believed in me, what kind of man would I be to spit on their nomination? "I accept."

Jason and I left our seats to join Argus when no one else voiced their opinion. We each stood alongside him as he spoke of his dreams for our pack's future, the new leader, and his hopes that we both gave it our all.

"We will conduct a series of three trials to occur without prior warning. You will not be given time to prepare, nor will you be allowed... help or interference," Argus said. He laid down the rules, placing stipulations that required us to pass at least two challenges.

And if we tied, it would come down to a fight. Like most shifters, I picked up muscle easily, but Jason's build put my body to shame. He had the whole Cro-Magnon look going on, from his sloped forehead to his gorilla-like arms. Ceres and I called him a knuckle-dragger behind his back.

"Then our business tonight is over, and it's time to hunt. We have a coyote invasion to nip in the bud."

Coyotes meant a fight and there was nothing we werewolves liked more than a good hunt. While the other pack members undressed and removed their clothes, Ceres and Daphne whispered a few feet to my rear. Straining didn't help me pick up much more than Jason's name and the word "shithead" so I abandoned the effort and pulled off my shirt.

"Thomas." Argus' voice turned me his direction.

"Yes, sir?"

Argus pulled me aside, away from the others, and stared me down. It was terrifying to be on the receiving end of his stern gaze. "Welcome to the family, son. I always knew she'd come around."

The breath I had been holding whistled out of me in one big exhale. "T-thanks. It was kind of sudden."

"And long overdue. Now... Ceres told me about your mishap with Craig."

Shit. Once a few awkward moments passed between us, my racing heart calmed. Maybe he sensed my terror, because he only grinned and waited, exuding the usual patience he displayed with the cubs.

"He struck Ceres and disrespected me, sir." Forcing even and deep breaths staved off the natural inclination to hyperventilate. I had to keep my cool.

"Tell me about it."

"He was intoxicated and high when he showed up. We fought, and he didn't give me much of a choice. I… broke one of the rules and killed in my house." After uttering the damning words, he should have bounced me right from the pack, but he didn't. His patience could be limitless; maybe that was another alpha trait Jason lacked. "So I called a raven to come clean up the mess."

"Good job."

I stared at him in stunned silence. "Thanks?" finally creaked from my lips.

"You showed good initiative in calling a raven. I'm impressed, son. Sometimes we don't have the luxury of a choice regarding where we make a kill. What matters most is that we handle the situation with dignity and responsibility. Thank you for looking out for my daughter."

Out of the corner of my eye, a pale wolf moved across the grass toward the tree line. Ceres turned her head to watch us closely.

"You're welcome, sir. I'd do anything for Ceres."

He patted me on the shoulder again before moving away to join his wife. Once the rest of my clothes were tossed over the back of a lawn chair, I dropped to all fours and loped across the expansive yard to join my mate.

It was time to prove my worth to the pack and show them I had what it took to lead.

CHAPTER 8

~THOMAS~

During my coffee break, Harrison called me into his office for a private chat about the current word on the street. I knew gossip would spread, but it never occurred to me that half the shifting world would know I was up for the role of Alpha.

If I wanted to be the Alpha, I needed a less demanding job with more flexible hours. I loved the Corbeau family, Harrison was my bro and my wingman at the club, but their pay sucked for the hours I put in. Besides, what kind of Alpha would I be if my greatest career accomplishment was that one time I told someone to upgrade their graphics driver? To be like Argus, I needed a real job with advancement opportunity, and this was a family business.

Harrison didn't want me to go, because it would be the end of our fun: no more goofing off on the clock in his office. With a dozen resumes with my name on it from here to Austin, someone had to eventually give me a call.

"Wow, man. Alpha. That's pretty big shit there."

"Tell me about it. Of course, I'm up against that shithead Jason."

"So, what happened? I don't have details yet." He offered me a Rockstar from his mini-fridge.

"Ceres nominated me, and I still don't know why. I think she planned it. She left early that day and wouldn't tell me why."

"Ask her."

"She won't talk about it. When I asked... well..." The distraction of her naked body had thrown me off the trail.

After claiming my long overdue blowjob, I fucked her until she could barely walk. I woke up to Ceres nestled beside me in bed, her furry head tucked beneath my throat. I couldn't remember the last time I slept as a wolf, but with her, it felt as natural as breathing and we had shifted just prior to falling asleep.

"We need to celebrate then."

"Hell no."

"C'mon, Tommy. Come out and have fun with us. You never leave the damn house these days."

I gestured around me, indicating the office. "You were saying?"

Our friend Bobby popped in and took a canned energy drink from the mini-fridge. Like a couple of the dudes in our small crowd, he knew me and Harrison weren't human. I shifted once during a guys' hunting trip for wild boar after Harrison got me wasted and dared me to do it. It would have been serious trouble for me if it wasn't a close-knit group.

"I overheard most of that, and I gotta say, you never leave the house unless it's to come to work, bruh," Bobby said.

"He has a point, dude," Harrison agreed. He cracked open and chugged his drink, as if the high caffeine content and taurine would remedy his apparent hangover. "You don't even play ball with us anymore. Do we need to change from b-ball to fetch to get you to participate?"

"I don't have the time to play ball, man." My friends meant well, but none of them were under the same pressure as me. I had less than a month to pass the most rigorous test of my entire life, and I couldn't even study for the exam.

"Anyway, word on the street is that your smoking hot roomie is single again. What's up with her and Craig?" Bobby asked.

Harrison glanced at me out of the corner of his eye.

"I dunno, maybe he went across the border for drugs and didn't come back," I suggested. Harrison snorted and glanced at me.

"Yeah, man. He's probably enjoying some deep sea fishing on a boat or hitting the surf," Harrison added.

"Is Ceres freaking out? Is that why you've been strained lately?" Bobby asked.

"I have a lot on my mind that doesn't have anything to really do with her," I explained. "The real estate taxes kicked my ass this year, and I'm working out a repair budget and schedule. And it's goddamned hot," I complained. "The couple in the house over on Mason Street is bitching again about the heat."

"Christ. That sucks, man," Bobby said. "Nice try changing the subject though. I give that attempt an eight out of ten."

Fuck! I gnashed my teeth and silently swore at him, calling my pal every dirty name in the book.

"Oh ho ho! Look at his face, Bobby."

"Spill it."

"Okay. Fine. Fuck both of you for making me say this: I bonded with Ceres."

"Uh, what's that mean?" Bobby asked.

"It means he dicked her and they're wolf-married," Harrison explained. Bobby's eyes became saucer wide behind his glasses. "How'd you get Ceres to accept you after all this time?"

"It started happening a while back, okay? Douchebag hit her, I did the usual and took care of her. One thing led to another." It wasn't too far from the truth.

"You know. I saw him and another dude fucking her once at a party."

Harrison and I turned to stare at Bobby. It was hard to determine what was most shocking, that he went to a party, or that he had owned up to voyeuring my then-roommate.

"What? I go to parties sometimes."

I didn't like the thought of any of my pals seeing Ceres that way, but I had to know more. "What the *fuck*, Bobby? How am I just hearing about this shit?"

"I almost forgot about it, to be honest. I was drunk, man. I stumbled past some bedroom in the frat house, and there she was. Craig even invited me to join in, but she looked too drunk… and I couldn't do that to you, bro."

Bobby was a good friend. I'd thank him later, but for now I dropped my face into one palm and groaned. My mate had a history of making poor decisions. Fuck, I was probably one of them, but at least shit like that wouldn't happen anymore on my watch. I'd die before I let someone take advantage of her.

An hour later, I snuck away and clocked out under Harrison's nose, but he fired a passive aggressive text message that arrived as I parked my truck.

I'd make it up to them later.

"Hi, Tommy! Look what I made!"

Jamie's excited cry made me turn and look down the drive. His mom's car had just pulled up and he hopped out from the back seat. The kid pounded down the sidewalk and stumbled to a halt before he crashed into my legs. I reached out to steady him as his mother followed a few steps behind.

Emma's work uniform showcased a body meant for Renaissance artwork. She wore a tidy, white blouse that stretched taut over her bust, but with the top button unfastened, and her turquoise pendant drew my eyes down to her cleavage. A fitted black pencil skirt clung to her hips, accentuated her waist, and made her ass seem even rounder. I would have killed to get ahold of it as she bent over.

Emma and Ceres were worlds apart, contrasting women of equally beautiful qualities. My bondmate was slim, tall, blonde, and athletic, the antithesis to Emma's petite and curvy frame.

I'd thought bonding with Ceres would dull my attraction to my friendly neighbor, but it only worsened it. Emma's close proximity stirred my blood.

"What's that, pal?" I focused on Jamie so I'd stop eyeballing his mom. Baseball stats became my internal mantra.

Jamie brandished a wooden boat for my appraisal.

"Nice," I told him. I turned the boat over in my hands a few times. The kid needed to work on his sanding, but he had the overall shape down to perfection. According to our last conversation, he wanted to learn to be good with his hands like me and build his mother a house one day.

"I still need to paint it then Mom says we can go sail it at the creek."

"Maybe I'll work on one of my own and we can call it a race." I grinned at him.

"Really? Awesome!"

Emma gave me the usual courteous greeting. "Good evening, Tommy. Sorry about the enthusiastic welcome. C'mon, kiddo, we need to get you cleaned up if you want to help make dinner."

"Mom makes the best beef pot pie," he boasted with pride. "You should have some. Can he have dinner with us, Mom? I can show him my paints!"

"Tommy and Ceres are more than welcome to come over if they don't have plans."

"Uh." I glanced at Ceres' shuttered bedroom window, a reminder of the things awaiting me behind it. Prior to leaving for work, I'd given her strict orders to follow and she'd flip her shit if I didn't return on time. Ceres had also offered to help me spice up my resume, otherwise pot pie would have been amazing. "Sorry, Jamie. I have to finish some job applications," I explained. It wasn't too far from the truth.

"Awww," Jamie lamented. "Well… okay. Hope we can play again soon."

"Another time," Emma said. She smiled down at her son then turned the cheery expression on me. "Invitation is always open if you two want chaotic company."

"Tomorrow night for sure. Come and get me if I forget."

After a parting wave, I went into my house and locked the door behind me. Not that I needed to. Not only did we live in a safe town, but I dared someone to break in while I was home. *Dared* them. Us wolves were stronger than we appeared, and our accelerated healing and enhanced reflexes made us deadly.

It was a big night for Ceres and me, filled with plans to discuss where our relationship was headed and what to do if I became the Alpha. Before I left for work, I'd even told her to be naked and waiting for me when I came home with dinner.

For the first time in all of our friendship, she obeyed me. I reached our living room to find my naked girlfriend spread across the sofa in a seductive pose that placed one of her long legs propped over the couch arm. She even wore the leather collar I bought her.

It looked good against her sandy hued fur.

"You're such a smart ass," I muttered. Ceres hopped down from the couch and padded to me. I crouched down to meet her eye to eye and run my fingers through her thick pelt. I kissed the tip of her dark nose. "You look beautiful."

She did. Ceres was a breathtaking wolf, and under the moonlight none of the other bitches in our pack compared. And once I claimed my title as Alpha of the sister pack, I could elevate her as my co-leader. It was a plan to strive for.

"Now shift back, babe. Don't make me wait."

After I straightened, Ceres rose from her wolf form and stood in a demure pose with her hands clasped behind her back. It put emphasis on her bare breasts, and not one to miss an opportunity, I dipped my head down to kiss one tit.

"Mm… welcome home," she greeted me.

Loosening the collar to fit it around her lupine neck meant it was too large for her as a human. I removed it and set it aside.

"I thought we might go for a run later tonight." I brought it up and nipped her sensitive nipple between my teeth. After I lashed it with my tongue, I exhaled warm air over the wet skin. Her fingers cradled the back of my head and held me close.

"I'd like that… I miss running with you, Tommy."

"I know. And I miss hunting with you. You make it easy."

Ceres' throaty laugh never failed to warm my heart. "Bullshit. You're the better tracker. You don't need me."

"I may not need you, but I want you," I replied. "Besides, how many times do I have to tell you that you're the faster wolf?" Color rose in her cheeks, undeniable and genuine pleasure. "And I also want dinner." Without another kiss or playful tease, I left our embrace and walked away to fetch a couple blankets from the linen closet. Once those were spread over the floor, we settled down for dinner in front of the television, both naked as the day we were born. We lay with full bellies and accepted the distraction of a romantic comedy, wrapped in each other's arms.

"Tommy?"

"Hm?"

Our spooned position meant that her ass cradled my dick perfectly. Golden blonde hair tickled my chest, skimmed over my naked skin, and made me resist the urge to seize a handful of it to guide her head down to blow me instead. Watching a movie was more than a date night — it was a battle of wills, hers against mine, my desire against her increasing arousal. I smelled her from the moment I stripped to join her on the blanket, and it brought me no small amount of pleasure to know she wanted me too.

"You have a really big cock."

I busted out laughing. Of all the things she could have said, I expected her to accuse me of dawdling or spout out another tease. The arm resting around her slim waist shifted to place my palm against her small tit. I cradled the perfect handful and rolled my thumb over the stiff tip.

"Thanks. I guess. Just realizing that?" I first saw Ceres naked a couple weeks after my sixteenth birthday. That day, she and her mother volunteered to take me for a run when Argus' business dealings ruined our guy plans. Back then, I was still shy and clinging to the human ideals of modesty, too used to her father teaching me. The two beautiful women had shed their clothes then waited for me to do the same.

"Mm... No. I used to think maybe you should have been a horse shifter instead."

By the time my laughter subsided, she had turned to face me and slid one leg over my hip, aligning our bodies until the tip of my cock slid over her waxed folds.

"Fuck me, Tommy. I can't pay attention to this terrible movie with your cock poking me in the ass."

"Maybe I want to watch the movie."

I really didn't. Dicking her would beat out a boring romcom any day, but I had a point to make.

"Turn back around."

"But—"

"Turn around," I repeated, sharper this time.

She grumbled and rolled over slowly, her body positioned forward just enough to separate us. If she planned to act like a spoiled child, the only alternative left to me was to treat her like one. I spanked her ass and left a red palm print against her skin before dragging her back close.

"Are you going to punish me?" she asked, coyly whispering. Dinner wasn't enough to sate all of my appetite. After kneeling beside her, I dragged her over my lap by a handful of hair, then wrapped it around my fist for good measure. I squeezed and kneaded her porcelain ass. Ceres was perfection, and she didn't even realize it. Athletic and slim, but plump enough in all the right places, just enough to show my girl loved Shiner, pizza, and Mexican takeout.

My palm cracked against her bottom hard enough for Ceres to flinch. Her breath quickened and she squirmed against my leg. She wriggled and spread her legs, an unvoiced plea for more.

Her fingers crept toward her snatch, where I intercepted them and delivered a stinging slap against her bald lips. She twisted left and right, writhing in protest and pleasure, but I held her hands out of my way. She wasn't allowed to finger herself.

I reduced her to incomprehensible babble with a few touches. At some point, she pleaded, "Please, Tommy, please."

At that moment, it wasn't about fucking and raw, no-holds barred sex. I abandoned all pretenses of being the dominant figure, the Alpha-in-Training, or even her best friend Thomas. I was just another man making love to a woman I adored with all of my heart. She was everything I wanted. Everything I needed.

When it was over and I held her close, I watched her struggle with her words.

"Look, Tommy... I-it's—"

I didn't rush her. She'd bared her body to me and given me something special, and in return, I granted time to sort through her equally tumultuous feelings. If she felt even a fraction of the feeling for me that I felt for her, then her silence was justified. "I'm glad we did this."

"So am I." I buried my face in her hair and breathed her in. I loved her.

CHAPTER 9

~CERES~

The night was perfect for a run. A few scattered clouds drifted across the sky and occasionally blocked out the pale crescent hanging above us. We didn't need a full moon to shift the way the legends and stories tell it.

The local wildlife sensed our presence and fled for their hiding places. We hadn't even abandoned our human bodies yet, but the squirrels scurried across the dark backyard, racing for the trees.

"Shhh," I giggled. "Neighbors are still awake. What if they see us?"

The lights were on at Emma's place, despite the late hour. I wasn't worried about being spotted, not from this distance, but Tommy didn't know that.

"They'll only see your lily white ass then," he shot back to me. With the door pulled shut behind us and our emergency key buried beneath the rose bushes, we were safe to frolic and run.

"Maybe she needs to see yours. From what she told me, it'll be the hottest thing she's seen since her son was born," I teased. Before he could swat me, I took off running across the grass, barefoot and free.

Tommy shifted first and overtook me in a few bounds. I passed him seconds later on my faster legs, then we leapt the fence side by side and sprinted into the green pastures. We loped through the heavy growth, playing and sometimes nipping each other. At least a couple hours had passed by the time we turned back for the house and shook off the brambles and bits of leaf from our furry coats.

Shifting back into my human form felt like losing a part of myself. There were days I wished I could stay as my lupine self but then I thought about the sacrifices I'd have to make. Like burritos, pizza, beer... and sex. Well, I wouldn't be giving that up entirely, but according to some of the older shifters, sex in our animal forms didn't have anything on two-legger fucking. I believed it.

"Someone's pulling an all-nighter. Maybe she has a guy friend over." After my afternoon with Emma, I didn't believe that for a second, but I watched Tommy's face for his reaction.

"Hmm?"

"Emma. Our hottie MILF next door is still awake. I said maybe she's got a date or something." A sniff of the air told me otherwise. The only people I smelled from the house next door were Emma and Jamie.

"So what if she did?"

I skipped to the rose bush and dug out the key. "Then she'd be taken and you'd have to stop checking out her ass."

"I don't check out her ass," he muttered under my breath.

"Sure you do, and I'm not complaining, Tommy." Opening the door, I led the way inside. "It'd do you both some good to have a romp."

"I'm... huh?"

"I mean, if you want to be an alpha, start thinking like one.

"What the fuck does screwing another woman have to do with being an alpha? Your dad doesn't go around banging other women."

A sigh escaped before I could muffle it. "He'd like you to think that."

"What do you mean?"

"Dad told me once, in a rare drunken confession, that he and mom aren't bonded. I mean, obviously they're mates, but not soul mates. I, uh, saw one of the omegas leaving his room once, one night when I was still living at home." And their unhappy marriage had colored my perception of relationships ever since. "Seeing them is why I couldn't be with you before, Tommy. I didn't want to end up like that and resenting our life together."

"Damn. I had no idea." Tommy rubbed the back of his neck. "Ceres, that's them. Not us. What you and I have is different. It's real. Your wolf finally saw me, so that means we're fated and meant to be."

"I know, Tommy, and it is. But..."

"Then what is it? Cause the way I see it, we have something here, and now you're all cavalier about me dicking some other chick."

This wasn't how I wanted things to go. I panicked, ice cubes filling my veins as a twisting sensation squeezed my gut. "I'm just saying I wouldn't be pissed if you decided to, you know, have some fun with Emma if the mood struck you."

"Is that how you see it? Fun?"

"Aw, c'mon Tommy, don't be like that. You and I are never going to change. *Ever.*"

"If you're trying to get me to go off and fuck her so you can do the same thing to some other guy, forget it."

"Tommy, *no.* That's not what I wanted at all."

He didn't hang around to hear the rest of my protests, and I knew better to follow until he got his temper under control. It took all of my willpower to wait outside the bathroom and to only enter after his shower was running.

I spied his shadow beyond the semi-translucent shower door.

"Tommy? Hey, I'm sorry. I didn't mean to piss you off."

"Not pissed," he replied.

I slid open the door despite his curt tone and stepped inside with him. "I wasn't trying to push you away. Please don't hate me."

"I don't hate you, but I'm not in the mood to have sloppy seconds after another Craig."

"Just hear me out and let me talk this time, okay? It's not about fucking another guy."

"Then what, Ceres? Huh? *What?*"

"It's Emma," I whispered. "While we were out, I felt the same sort of draw toward her as I did when we were on the couch. It felt like... my wolf saw her."

Tommy stiffened against me when I pressed close to rest my hands on his shoulders. "You, too?"

"*Yes,* Tommy. Yes, me, too. That's what I've been wanting to tell you." My heart swelled with elation and profound relief, mirrored on his own handsome face as he sagged against the shower tiles.

"I thought something was wrong with me. I thought I was losing it that I could barely keep control around her some days. That I didn't deserve you anymore."

"No, Tommy," I insisted. "We both feel for her. Something changed after my wolf recognized yours, and now we can both see Emma."

"What do we do?" His arms encircled me, holding me in a reassuring embrace. I turned my cheek against his shoulder. "Do we wait for it to pass?" he asked.

"We could make her ours?" The words escaped in a hope-filled question.

"But how? Why would she even want to?"

Men. Honestly. "Baby, she likes you. You've been blind all this time while chasing me, but she *likes* you."

"So what are you telling me to do, Ceres? Fuck her when I've barely had the chance to get to know her?"

"I'm telling you to follow your wolf and go with your instinct. Be the alpha I know you are, Tommy."

~THOMAS~

The promise of an evening thunderstorm cooled the summer day and blew a breeze across the porch. I lazed shirtless on the swing with Ceres' e-reader on my lap, lost in a newly released space opera. Occasional gusts of rain misted through the mosquito screen, a relaxing sensation after recent days of dry weather.

Emma's beat up sedan cruised past my home and pulled into her driveway. She popped the trunk and rushed an armload of groceries to the porch then fumbled with her keys.

There's my chance. Now or never. I sprinted over to help, taking a load of bags from her open trunk in passing. We met face to face as she was coming out the door for the next armful.

"Oh my God!" Emma leapt back with both hands lifted to her heart.

"Sorry, it looked like you could use a hand before the downpour really starts."

"No, it's okay. You just startled me..."

I caught her checking out my chest and bit the inside of my cheek to maintain a straight expression. Ceres was right. I was a blind fool. "I'll get the rest."

"Are you sure?"

"Go on, it's no problem." I put a hand at her hip and turned her around, sending her off with a little nudge. Rain slicked my hair down over my forehead and my ears by the time I made it into the house to join her in the kitchen. Emma fetched me a bath towel and I remained acutely aware of the path her eyes took all the while I dried off. She seemed to watch every drop of water with her breath held.

"I wasn't planning to cook since Jamie is with my aunt this weekend, but I don't mind if you'd like to stay for dinner. Ceres told me she'd be at the clinic today."

"Hey, if you've got a day off from being a mom, you really don't have to cook for me."

"Believe me, you're not making any trouble. I have to put these away before stuff begins melting, but make yourself at home. There's juice and sweet tea in the fridge if you want. Or beer."

"You like beer? I thought you had the same taste for margaritas and frou-frou drinks as Ceres."

Emma's dimples made an appearance. "I do when the mood strikes. Not to support all those Native American stereotypes or anything, but sometimes when Jamie's asleep or gone for the weekend, I like to relax with a drink."

"Hey, I'm not judging. You saw my liquor cabinet."

About twenty minutes later, we settled on the couch while the storm raged outside. We watched the latest action flick featuring cops on an adventure to solve a series of murders in a big city overwhelmed by drugs.

"This reminds me… the cops were by this morning asking about that guy who went missing."

"Ugh. Craig."

"Yeah. Not that I had much to tell them. I didn't know the guy, you know? I mean, yeah, I saw him a few times when he'd come around with Ceres on his bike but that's it."

"He never bothered you did he?"

"Not really. Mostly he was just loud. You know, revving up at god awful hours."

Emma tucked her legs up beneath her. She had great calves, probably due to all the standing and walking in the kitchen at her job, and I wanted to nibble her thick thighs. The contrast between them and Ceres' lean legs turned me on as much as the cleavage spilling from the top of her navy blue V-neck.

God, I wanted to fuck those tits. I wanted to make friends with her first and bond on a non-physical level, but my wolf had his own plans. Ignoring the hard-on stiffening beneath my damp shorts, I focused on the movie and let our conversation gradually shift back to the action.

It was difficult, especially since I could smell the pheromones coming off her skin. Somehow, we ignored our mutual attraction and chatted over reheated bacon cheeseburger meatloaf, snickerdoodles, and Shiner. We split the last bottle in her fridge, passing it back and forth and taking turns. Her mint chocolate chip lip gloss left a sweet ring on the bottle's rim, a pleasant tingle I wanted to experience by kissing her instead.

Emma became quieter during the gritty action scenes than the numerous moments of tit and ass, making awkward conversation whenever one of the leading ladies stripped on the screen, as if compelled to fill the silence.

God forbid a man and woman watch a few seconds of choreographed breast jiggling together without it turning into a blush-fest. Still, her embarrassment was a little endearing. Ceres would have grabbed her boobs and compared tit sizes.

"Sounds like it's letting up outside. At least the thunder stopped." Emma moved to the window and peeked between the blinds. A dismal and cloudy gray sky continued to drizzle on the sidewalk.

"Yeah, maybe I should head home now."

"Oh, yeah, I guess that's a good idea. The storm will probably pick up again." Her expression fell a little, broadcasting her disappointment. She forced the brief frown away with a sunny smile. "Thank you again for helping with the groceries."

"Nah. It's cool. All the times you've brought me cookies, brownies, and chili? I can carry bags in for a friend."

"If you didn't help me eat brownies I'd be a whale," she laughed. "I'm already fat enough."

"Fat? Huh?" She jerked me out of my daydream, in which both of her toned calves were over my shoulders while she writhed on the bed in front of me, naked, those gorgeous and full tits quivering each time I made her moan. Fuck. "You're not fat."

Emma shrugged and stacked up our plates. "Eh, it's alright. I've never been a stick and after Jamie, well, my body just isn't what it used to be, I guess."

"Emma, you look great. Trust me when I tell you that there's nothing wrong with your size."

"You're sweet, Tommy, thanks. Still, I'd kill to have a figure like Ceres'."

"Between you and me, she was bitching the other day about wanting boobs like yours." Ceres would murder me if she knew I told.

Laughter filled the room. The husky quality of her voice caused another twitch in my shorts. "Really? I'd totally give her some if I could. Big breasts are overrated."

Before I could tell her breasts were great at any size, Emma surprised me with a hug. Her arms became a warm presence around me, an impulsive embrace that pressed her curvy body close and enveloped me in the subtle scent of brown sugar and sweet almond. I hugged her back and prayed she didn't feel my stiff dick nudging her belly.

"Don't be a stranger. I know you two usually take care of yourselves but if you ever need anything, feel free to knock." She gestured toward the plates on the coffee table. "We always have leftovers."

"Thanks... Uh, should I help you clean that up?"

"If you touch a single thing, I'll kick your ass."

I held up both hands. "Whoa. Okay. No helping clean. Got it."

"You're my guest, and a welcome one at that." She walked with me to the door and peeked her head outside. "Want to borrow my umbrella?"

"Nah, I'll be good. A little rain never hurt anyone."

I returned home to find Ceres opening and closing cabinets in the kitchen.

"Uuugh... We have nothing to eat. Tommy, why didn't you buy groceries?"

"Because you're every bit as capable of going shopping as I am," I pointed out.

"I was gone all day and where the hell were you?"

"Ended up watching a movie with Emma after the storm started up."

"Yeah?" Ceres raised both brows. "Boy, you move fast." She glanced at my shirtless chest and raised both brows suggestively.

"Do I smell like I just had sex?"

"No, unfortunately." Her smile flattened, taking on a strange look. "Do you think she likes me? Normally, I can tell if I have a shot with a girl but... I can't read Emma. What if she doesn't have any interest in me?"

"Ceres, baby, look." I took her face between both of my hands and leaned down to kiss her. "We're a package deal. Me and you both. Got that? We'll see

where she stands on the idea and if she's open to…
trying this with us. It feels right and I don't think our
wolves would steer us wrong."

She gave me a weak, uncertain smile and leaned
up to take another kiss. "You're right. So should I
assume you smell like cookies and beer because you
ate dinner with her?"

"Yep. But you're in luck because she has
leftovers, and I think—" I peeled her off of me and
turned her around, guiding her with my next steps to
the door. "—she'd appreciate your company, too."

We spent the next few days balancing time with
Emma. Sometimes we courted her alone and
sometimes together as a couple, befriending her
before we dared to take the next step. On Emma's
next day off, the three of us caught a horror movie
together. I was forced to sit between the two women
as they clung to me and often poked fun if I jumped,
too.

We chose not to hide our relationship from
Emma, realizing complete honesty was imperative to
gaining her trust. We couldn't build a new relationship
based on a lie. She seemed genuinely happy to hear
we'd sorted out our trouble, and that was how I knew
without a doubt that Emma was the girl to complete
our triad. Not to exclude Jamie, I carried on no
differently than I did before my attraction for Emma
blossomed — I took him out for pizza and a dinosaur
flick while the girls visited the salon for fresh haircuts.

"Tommy, do you think dogs are better than cats?"
"Dogs are superior in every way," I replied.
"But Ceres has a cat."
"Ceres is a weirdo."

"I want a dog, but Mom says I can't have one because of my asthma, and I don't want a dumb hairless cat."

I knew where he was heading before we got there. Sighing, I glanced over at the kid in the passenger seat. "Did you already find a dog you want?"

"I did some research," he admitted. "And I've been saving my allowance."

Smart kid. Researching and saving. I grinned at him and pulled into the driveway. "I'll mention it to her. Maybe if I finish those plans to put up a fence around your place, she'll be more receptive to the idea."

"Thanks, Tommy."

A couple days later, I walked out of an interview in Austin with a job offer. I'd never felt more in control of my life. Ceres texted me on the way home with a request for me to bring fast food, so I stopped at the local diner to fetch our supper. She claimed to be helpless after a dose of Tylenol 3 for her cramps following a day on her feet in the clinic. Empathizing with her bedridden plight, I promised to bring her a slice of warm apple pie and told her to stay in bed.

"Good evening, Tommy. You sure are dressed up awfully nice, son." Mrs. Mabel Gentry, the kind and elderly owner of my favorite diner, smiled at me from behind the counter.

I smoothed the front of my shirt. Opportunities to dress nicely with a tie were few and far between. "I just came from a job interview in the city, ma'am."

"Such a fine young man. They'll be lucky to have you, Tommy."

"Thanks." An automatic rush of heat surfaced to my cheeks. I liked to hang around in her diner sometimes for chitchat. My gram and Mrs. Mabel had been close friends, and I'd been sampling her pies for years as a child and later as a teen. Nowadays I had to force her to take my money. "I thought I'd celebrate with whatever's on the special tonight."

"It's whatever you want to be on the special tonight, Tommy. Tonight's your night, and I just won't take no for an answer."

I placed an order for two chicken fried steak dinners and she threw in half an apple pie on the house. "You're the best, Mabel. Where's Adam? You never work on Wednesdays." It was the one day of the week Mabel took off like clockwork. She generally closed on Sundays for church.

"He's down with the flu. How's that pretty girl doing?"

"Ceres graduated, ma'am. She's working at a veterinary clinic out of town now a few days a week."

"Tell her I said congratulations. No wonder I haven't seen her in here in so long." She passed me a tall cup of sweet tea over the counter, one of those things she'd probably neglect to charge me for. To balance that, I'd stuff all of the change she gave me back into the tip jar.

"I will, ma'am. Thanks." Like I needed a drink when I was about to burst after a day of driving and chatting up people for a job.

A foreign, unpleasant scent wafted to me on the breeze and made my wolf's hackles raise. A giant of a man entered the diner. A smarter bear shifter would have skipped through town since their kind and mine tended to clash with impunity. Atropos was wolf territory.

"Evening stranger," Mabel greeted, kind and welcoming as ever. "What can I get for you? Hi Pam, hi Jack, I'll be with you in a second."

I waved to the young woman and boy entering the diner.

"Hi Tommy!" Jack called. "Are you comin' to my birthday?"

"Sure am, kiddo. Couldn't keep me from it."

I ducked into the back to use the restroom and returned moments later to hear raised voices. Fear was a palpable presence in the air, one my hyper-senses picked up the moment I opened the bathroom door. Keeping close to the wall, I edged forward and peeked around the corner. The werebear had a gun trained on Mabel, then he swung his arm around and aimed the weapon at the rest of the customers. Pam had Jack behind her to shield her son from harm. The kid was petrified.

"Throw your fucking purses on the table. Your wallet too, old man. Nice and slow... yeah. Empty your pockets and turn 'em inside out."

At the sight of my community in trouble, fury took the wheel and pounded my pulse to a fevered rhythm. The loyal wolf in me couldn't stand idly by, hiding in the restroom corridor while some thug ran off with Mabel's hard-earned money.

It was only money. So what if the guy left with a couple wallets and her daily wages? Someone at church would probably take up a collection plate to help Mabel. Pam made decent money as a teacher. But the two old men in the back... one of them was a 'Nam vet living on a close pension. Whatever he lost, no matter how little, was going to hurt him.

Most of all, the territorial wolf in me couldn't stand there and let it happen. This was my town.

Just as certainly as I smelled and identified him on entrance, I was sure he recognized me as well. I couldn't rely on absolute stealth — instead, I hoped he wouldn't realize I'd returned from the john with every intention of fucking him up. The element of surprise was my only chance.

"You think I care? Tell that old biddy to empty her register and give me everything before I plug a hole in her," the bear raged at one of the customers. He glanced to the corner where Pamela huddled with Jack to console him. "Tell that brat to shut the fuck up!" When he whirled, he turned the gun on the kid. His mother screamed and clutched him harder, blubbering apologies and pleas for him to leave her child alone.

Was I quick enough to take on a lone gunman? I wished for Ceres' speed and unmatched reflexes. I had strength on my side, a small benefit when up against a bear shifter in his human form. The guy had muscles on top of his muscles and a good six inches on me. He didn't need a gun to scare Mrs. Mabel. One look at her pale features and panicked breathing set me into action, flying across the diner's tiled floor.

I crashed into him and pitted my strength against his muscular arm to knock the handgun's aim toward the floor. At least then, if he pulled the trigger out of surprise, it would glance off the linoleum instead. After that, I twisted his wrist with my right hand, bringing my left fist down into the middle of his forearm in a bid to shatter a couple bones. The handgun slid across the floor. A broken arm didn't make a bear defenseless. It made them angrier.

My opponent was too large to be anything but a grizzly. His skin stretched taut over his obscenely large muscles, his neck too thick for me to get him into a sleeper hold. I could have leapt on his back and tried to choke him out, but there wasn't any space to fit my arm. Fuck.

Mabel screamed my name as he crashed me into a table. The back of my skull exploded in pain and white spots bloomed in my vision. He hit like a freight train. Worse, his feral musk called to my inner beast. I wanted to shred him to pieces for what he'd done.

No, no, no. I couldn't shift in front of all these people. Over a half dozen innocent faces would bear witness to the change if I allowed it to overtake me, and if I fell into the frenzy now, there was no guaranteeing I wouldn't hurt one of them, too. I had to keep it calm. I had to keep cool. Couldn't let another Craig happen.

I suppressed the pain and struck back at my assailant, slamming my palm against his nose. The satisfying crack was accompanied by a squirt of blood and a pained bellow. I used the distraction and rolled off the Formica table then aimed a kick at his knee joint. The bear went down, assisted by my helpful dive onto his back.

He was bigger, but I was faster. Before he could recover, I used his heavier weight to my advantage and flipped him onto the floor. With his beefy arm trapped between my knees, it didn't take much effort to dislocate it.

Thank you, Uncle Ian. Those military grappling moves had finally come in handy during a fight.

"You fucker!" the bear screamed from the floor, ready to stagger to his feet when I rolled away from his other reaching arm.

I cracked the diner chair over his head. He went out like a light and slumped over the floor while wide-eyed spectators stared.

"Tommy, are you okay?"

"Yeah, I'm good." Once the initial disorientation passed, the blurry world around me came into focus and I glanced around at their concerned faces. I hadn't died, and I hadn't shifted — all in all it felt like a success.

"Someone tie him up until the police get here! Get his gun!" The others went into action to help, while someone guided a chair behind me.

"Here, sit down. You look out of it, son."

Transitioning from man to beast came as easy as breathing, but fighting off an involuntary shift drained me. I wanted to sleep and rest off the body aches from the fight.

"Police are on the way, son. What you did just now was outstanding. Just simply outstanding," Mr. Porter praised me. "Didn't know you could fight like that, Thomas. You should've gone into the marines like I told ya." I heard this from Mr. Porter at least once a month. He was a die-hard believer that every man needed to join the service.

"Can't believe you did that," Mr. Miller said, leaning over to rest his hand on my shoulder. "Damned foolish and brave thing you did."

"Mama, is Tommy going to be okay?" Jack asked.

"I'm fine, Jack. Just a little bruised."

Mrs. Mabel approached with a bag of frozen peas in a Ziplock bag. She applied it to my face, her tender and grandmotherly touch bringing even more heat to my cheeks.

The cops arrived and took our statements. After the stress of dealing with them and repeating the story over and over, I was released from the scene to return home. Mrs. Mabel wouldn't allow me to pay for my order. I tried.

Juggling the order from the diner, I entered an eerily silent house. "Ceres?" When she didn't answer the call, I shut and locked the door behind me to limp into the kitchen. Pain radiated through my ribs, spreading over my torso like a blanket of agony. A quick glance beneath my t-shirt revealed mottled blue and purple.

I was lucky he didn't shatter my ribs. Groaning, I dropped the tough guy act and set our dinner on the table. Ceres skipped into the kitchen just as I pulled some ice from the freezer and wrapped the cubes in a towel.

"What happened to your face? Holy shit." She raised her fingers to my cheek and touched the dark bruise. "Are you all right?"

"Yeah, I'm good. Honestly, it looks worse than it is." Her fingers pressed against the tender spot on my cheek, making me hiss in a breath between my teeth.

"Oh yeah, it only looks worse, right? Do you want one of my Tylenol 3s?"

Ceres fretted over me like we were in grade school again.

"I brought you dinner and pie like you—"

"I can't believe you're worried about my pie! Oh my God, your face."

Maybe her over the top reaction could be chalked up to her time of the month. "It's only a bruise."

"What happened? I thought I heard police sirens earlier, but I was so sleepy I laid back down."

I described the incident in the diner, and all the while her eyes grew increasingly large until she threw her arms around my waist. If she embraced me any tighter, I would have pleaded for death.

"You went up against a man with a gun?!" she yelled.

"What else was I supposed to do? He was aiming at Mabel and swinging it around all over the place." I couldn't have lived with myself if he'd hurt someone and I could have prevented it.

"You don't seem to have any open wounds—"

"And I'll recover from the rest of it by tomorrow. I'll sleep it off."

My failed attempt to assure her ended with me without clothes and Ceres tucking me into her bed. According to her, I looked like shit.

~CERES~

Part of me was afraid Tommy had a concussion. He swore up and down he felt fine, never lost consciousness, and that I needed to see the other guy. If he wasn't a werewolf, I would have whisked him away to the ER in a heartbeat and had him assessed by a medical professional.

"But you *are* a medical professional. You're a doctor," Tommy reminded me, grinning in his sexy and lopsided way.

"I'm an animal doctor."

"I'm a werewolf," he pointed out.

"You're a smart ass," I fired back. "I mean it, Tommy. You stay in this bed and rest."

We had supper together in my bed once I reheated it. While he made every attempt possible to appear calm and collected, I knew him too well to be fooled. He was rattled, and I couldn't blame him.

I knew Tommy would face one of his trials at the diner when my dad phoned during my lunch break for a favor. Without any details, I'd assumed it would be something small and harmless, some kind of clever trick or issue requiring his intellect. Maybe I should have known better than to underestimate Dad's insidious mind.

While Tommy dozed off, I returned to my romantic novel. It had just reached the good part — a smoking hot sex scene between a handsome military commander and his lover — when my phone buzzed on the table. I plucked it up and swiped the screen to find a text from Dad. ETA five minutes. Great.

"Where you goin'?" Thomas asked drowsily when I began to slip out of bed. Returning my palm to his chest, my fingers ran over the finer, sparse black hairs and petted him. After another soothing stroke, his blue eyes closed again.

"Just downstairs to get a drink."

"Oo…" He snored again, drifting off before he could even finish the second syllable. Once my giggles were under control, I moved downstairs. Dad was always on time and the last thing I wanted was for him to ring the doorbell and wake Tommy up. So I grabbed an afghan and stepped outside to wait for him on the porch. His silver BMW pulled into the drive exactly five minutes after his text.

"You're swinging by awfully late." Not really. It was barely going on eight, but my parents didn't visit much unless it was time to chastise me for living my life the way I wanted. Or in my mom's case, she decided it was time to tell me I was a waste of her womb and a disappointment to her.

My father joined me on the porch and kissed my cheek. "Where's Thomas?"

"Asleep, Daddy. He really got worked over at the diner so I dosed him up on codeine and made him go to bed."

"Yes, so I heard. He handled the situation well."

He sounded so calm about it all. Maybe even a tad dismissive. "There was a kid there, Daddy. A *kid*. How could you send a bear in there to scare poor old Mabel? She could have had a heart attack."

At least he had the good grace to look mildly apologetic. "When I set this up with Mason I was under the impression Mrs. Gentry took the day off."

It gave me some comfort knowing my dad had actually considered something like that, but it didn't change the fact that he'd sent in a bear. Tommy had reeked of the stinky thing when he came home.

"Who's Mason?"

"An old associate," Dad replied. "He slipped away from custody an hour ago."

"Geez, Dad." The swinging bench squeaked as I settled onto it. Dad took the empty spot beside me. "Dusty was in on it?"

Dad kept a couple members of the local human law enforcement in his pocket for situations like these. Sheriff Dusty Haverton's authority gave him the freedom to look the other way. The rest of our small police department was entirely clueless and we liked to keep it that way.

"I handled it so don't worry about the details."

"Fine. But what about Tommy? Did he pass or not?"

Dad folded his arms and leaned back on the bench, a thoughtful expression on his face. My dad and I were as different as night and day when it came to physical features. My girlfriends in high school and later college used to joke that I had the hot dad, smitten by his distinguished appearance, his salt and pepper hair, and his youthful exuberance. The werewolf blood kept our kind younger longer.

"Jason failed his first trial. Your mother claims I stacked the test against him. She won't be happy that Thomas passed."

"What does she have against him? Daddy, I don't get it. She's always liked Thomas."

"I know." He sighed. "But this doesn't have anything to do with Thomas. You know I don't like to lie to you, and I won't about this, but..." He inhaled a deep breath.

"Daddy? What is it?"

"Your mom and Jason are fated. If he wins the new pack, she plans to part ways with me and go with him."

The news hit me like a cruel punch in the gut. I blinked at him, waiting for the punchline to the joke. "Mom is leaving you?"

"Yeah. Don't blame her too hard, punkin. I knew it was a risk when I first took over the pack and married her, that one day, one of us would find our other half."

"That doesn't excuse how she's treating this. She's trying to stack it in his favor because she doesn't want to step down as an alpha female! That's bullshit! Dad, can't you overrule her or something and just call an end to this? We both know Jason's no good. He'll run the pack into the ground then you'll have to salvage whatever's left. If his bad choices don't expose us."

Dad never lost his temper, a contrast between our personalities that once made me wonder if mom had an affair on the side. "I've said as much to her, Ceres, but if I cancel the contest, she'll only claim I'm doing it out of spite. At any rate, once he's awake and coherent, break the news to him. I'd hoped to talk to congratulate him, but at this point you'll suffice."

"Gee, thanks."

"Sorry, kid. If it alleviates your concerns in the least, know that I personally filled the gun with blanks prior to sending him into the diner."

"You were there?"

"Of course."

After Dad's full disclosure, he left me to handle the fallout with Tommy and drove off in his sporty BMW. One slice of apple pie later, I rejoined Tommy in bed and snuggled up to his side.

It seemed I had barely closed my eyes when a loud series of knocks jarred me awake. A quick glance at the clock revealed the time was close to midnight. Tommy hadn't budged, so I crawled from bed and hurried downstairs.

The last person I expected to see was the neighbor. Emma was soaked, trembling where she stood on the porch with her hand raised ready to knock again.

"Ceres, I'm so sorry to wake you. It's my sink. The faucet snapped and I can't get the water to turn off."

"I'll try to wake Tommy up. Shit." If I couldn't shake him out of his drug-induced stupor, I'd have to call his go-to emergency plumber. Tommy left a list of numbers on the fridge for me to use in the event of a complete catastrophe while he was away.

"I'm sorry," she apologized again. "I can try calling a plumber—"

"No, no. It's okay. He'll flip his shit if he finds out we didn't tell him."

CHAPTER 10

~THOMAS~

I staggered down the stairs after Ceres coaxed me into putting on a pair of boxers. Shaking off codeine was a slow process, and she'd doped me up with an above normal dose to get me to bed.

"Emma?"

Her expression changed when I stepped barefoot onto the porch.

"What happened to you?!"

"Stopped a robbery," I grumbled.

She fretted over me, despite being wet from the neck of her racerback nightshirt to the bottom. A useless layer of thin cotton clung to her full breasts, teasing me with the outline of her erect nipples.

"What the hell is going on with the sink?"

"I went in to get a drink and the faucet handle snapped off and water spewed everywhere and I can't get the shutoff valve to turn," she babbled in a frantic rush. "I threw down a bunch of towels."

A visual snapped into my mind, her screaming and flailing as water shot like a geyser from the faulty kitchen plumbing. The threat of water damage didn't ease my amusement.

"Calm down… we'll fix it."

"Are you laughing at me?"

"No. Never." After assurances were made and my tools were collected, we hurried across the massive lawn and into her single floor home where a disaster zone awaited us. Water continued to spurt at an alarming rate, splattering the tile behind the sink and soaking the window curtains above it. It spilled over the counter surface onto the floor, requiring me to navigate with care or bust my ass in front of my sexy tenant. I stole another look at her plump thighs. The wet, clinging fabric molded against her curves and perfectly outlined her figure. My mouth watered and the wolf in me craved the sight of her on her hands and knees, her round ass upraised and thighs parted. My human side wanted her beneath me as I sucked and nibbled her generous tits.

Damn, I needed to focus.

Thanks to her quick thinking and the towels, the kitchen floor wasn't the disaster zone it could have been, but a wrench and all of my werewolf muscle proved insufficient for budging the shut off valve. Until it snapped. The aging pipes disagreed with using supernatural strength.

"Shit!"

"What happened?" Emma returned with more towels and a blanket to throw down over the pooling water.

"Gonna have to turn off water for the whole house, Em. Sorry."

"I guess it's a good thing Jamie is with my aunt all week then so I can work."

A couple minutes later, we were both in the middle of her kitchen again, soaking up the spreading puddle with every bath towel she had. My attention drifted to her bottom each time she bent over, stiffening my dick until it ached. I didn't bother to hide it.

"I'll visit Home Depot to get some new parts tomorrow, okay? Don't worry about this. If you need to use the shower, I have a guest bath you can use before work."

"My hero," she laughed, turning to look at me. I took it like a man and gazed back at her long after her brown eyes swept down my chest to the hard outline pressing against my damp boxers. "Um… let me find you another dry towel."

"Emma, wait." My fingers encircled her wrist.

"Yeah?"

Something raw and animalistic came over me. It was like every bad porno I'd ever watched, hot and fast, a whirlwind of passion that began when I yanked Emma in close against me and claimed her mouth in an urgent kiss. At first, her fingers curled over my shoulders and her lips parted to exhale a breathy sigh.

Then she slapped me. Hard. Pain and heat spread across my unbruised cheek as she stepped back. "You're with Ceres!"

"I know how this seems, Emma, but it's okay. She doesn't mind." *Fuck. Why don't I ever think things through?*

"Excuse me?"

"Ceres and I are together, yes, but we have an agreement."

"You seriously expect me to believe she'd be okay with this? With us?" Emma's heart was still racing, her breasts heaving with each heavy breath.

"Come on, Emma. You know me. How long have I chased her? Do you think I'd do anything to fuck that up? I'm not asking you to sneak around behind her back. I'm not saying keep it a secret. I'm saying that we're both... seriously attracted to you." I took another step forward, only to pause when she tightened one fist.

"Both...?"

"Ceres likes you, Em. So do I. This was her idea." Honesty. One of the best traits of a strong alpha was honesty.

"I..."

"Do you want me, Emma? Say no and I'll never bother you with this again. It's all up to you."

For one terrifying moment, I thought she was going to kick me the hell out. Her gaze flickered between me and the door several times while she waged her own internal battle. Then she was in my arms with her mouth on mine. Emma's lower body grinded into me and our clothing failed as a barrier. One handful of her nightshirt hitched it up above her ass, baring the modest boy shorts beneath. I slipped my hand beneath them and squeezed.

"Hot damn, your ass is perfect." I wanted to delve right between those cheeks and fuck her right. She was built like a sex goddess, a Renaissance beauty with full curves.

One lift was all it took to place her up on the island counter.

Right there in that moment, I realized Ceres was right. Emma was our third and more than anything, I wanted to be the one who opened her eyes to the truth. To have her first and claim her for us both. Standing between Emma's legs with her arms around me, I was ready to make that plunge.

CHAPTER 11

~EMMA~

I was dreaming. I had to be. It was like waking up and finding myself in one of my favorite trashy romance novels where the hot guy falls for the average girl next door.

Tommy pulled my wet nightshirt up over my head and dragged my panties down until they dangled from my right ankle. His gaze raked over my body, alive with unconcealed hunger that tightened my nipples and made my body tingle from head to toe.

He mapped out my curves with his hands, squeezing my breasts and lowering his head to take one nipple between his lips. The electric current of pleasure shot through my body straight to my core.

"Fuck, you're beautiful." His mouth left one hardened nipple only to close around the other. His tongue flicks turned my insides to jelly, pooling undeniable heat in my belly. How long had I fantasized and watched while he chased his sexy roomie? Too long.

Cold laminate met my back and brought on another shiver. Tommy's warm palms massaged my breasts before moving down the rest of my body. He bent over me and traced the same path with his lips and teeth, breathing me in. Like a wild animal, his nose skimmed down my stomach and his teeth scraped against my navel.

"I've been wanting to do this for weeks, Emma." The husky growl in his voice raised the hair on the nape of my neck broke my skin out in excited goosebumps.

He hooked his arms under my legs and lifted my lower body. Before I could register his intentions, his face was between my thighs and his mouth was on me.

"Tommy!" Stars danced across my vision, even with my eyes shut. The man knew how to use his tongue and I writhed in his hold. "Fuck, I want... I want..."

He turned his mouth from my throbbing pussy and gave my thigh a sharp nip. The brief pain turned me on even more.

"Tell me, baby. Tell me what you want." He lowered my rump back to the counter and kissed his way up my body. A second playful nip found its place between my breasts and my entire body clenched.

"I need you inside me." I grasped at his shoulders, the broad muscle flexing beneath my fingertips. In his arms, I felt weightless, plucked from the counter too easily when he carried me through my home to the bedroom.

After laying me out on the queen sized mattress, he dropped on one knee between my spread legs. His fingers caressed the sensitive skin of my inner thighs and eventually found their way to my pussy. Two delved in, testing me, pumping, then coming away slick with my desire. He licked both digits and I melted.

"Mmm... Sweeter than I'd dreamed of."

Hot color swept up my neck into my face at his words. All this time I'd been fantasizing over him, he'd been doing the same. The knowledge emboldened me enough to sit up and peel his wet boxers down to his knees. His thick cock swayed, jutting out proudly from beneath his chiseled abs. I wanted to kiss every inch of his torso and taste him in my mouth.

So I indulged.

The fine hairs on his chest tickled my nose and chin as I sealed my mouth over one flat nipple. Flicking my tongue over the sensitive skin earned his pleased groan. Dragging my nails over his firm ass and down his thighs made him bump his hips forward, nudging his dick against my soft tummy.

"Goddamnit, Em, touch me. Please. Feel how much I want you."

Rather than give in to his request straight off, I worked my mouth up his chest instead. Each mottled bruise received the soft touch of my lips. I continued to lay the ascending line of kisses until I reached his ear.

"Tell me how much, Tommy," I whispered. "Tell me you've wanted me as much as I've wanted you."

"All I could think about when we hung out the other day was burying my cock inside of you, Em. No lie."

His words evoked new depths of passion within me. Without another word, I wrapped my hands around him and delivered a slow, testing stroke, but touching him wasn't enough.

Bowing down in front of him, I gave in to my desires and took his cock into my mouth. Tommy's hand grasped my hair, his fingers tightening in the damp strands when I sank down as far as I could take him. Giving blowjobs was a personal favorite activity. I loved the control it gave me. His balls were soft and filled my cupped hand. Each groan and muttered expletive that fell from Tommy's lips was music to my ears.

"Emma... oh shit... Emma, baby, no. As much as I want to fill that pretty mouth of yours I need to be inside of you. Right fucking now."

A tug on my hair and his desperate words brought me off of his dick, though I gave the flared head one last suckle to collect his salty-sweet precum. Tommy jerked my head back and kissed me savagely, with more passion than he'd shown so far. Our teeth gnashed together and our tongues tangoed in a dominant display. He tugged on my hair again until I had no choice but to lay back, his weight following me down this time.

Holy shit. I hadn't been exaggerating when I thought his dick was big. He cleaved into me with one solid stroke, stretching and filling my pussy until he was sunk full hilt and his balls slapped against my ass. And damn did it feel good. My lips parted from his and I cried out, my back arching and head falling back.

"Fuck, Emma, fuck," he rasped against my throat. His backstroke nearly parted our bodies, only for him to slam forward anew. It was primal. Raw. And god how I loved it.

"Harder, Tommy."

Muscles bunched and rolled beneath my fingertips on his back. I held him tightly, nails pressed hard against his skin. Each thrust was tireless and our mutual grunts and cries filled the room. Twice I felt his teeth against my throat. The third time I arched my neck back to give him more room, craving the hard scrape over my leaping pulse point.

"You like that, baby?"

"Yes," I cried out in response. "God I need you deeper."

"Just tell me what you want, Emma." He nipped my ear then suckled on the lobe. My pussy tightened, squeezing around him.

"I want to be on top of you, Tommy," I groaned. "I want to ride you so bad." I'd had the fantasy too many nights to pass up on the chance.

We rolled together, messing my blankets up even more. The moment he was beneath me, I drew my knees forward on either side of him and sat up, looking down into his handsome face and stunning blue eyes. They reminded me of rough, uncut sapphires, deep blue with honey-brown flecks. Above him, with his eyes drinking me in, I felt sexy and confident. Desired. There was no mistaking the lust and hunger in his eyes as he took in every inch of me.

As I rode him, Tommy's hips thrust up and down, burying his rigid dick between my swollen folds. He felt so good, so hard inside me, every fucking penetration better than the last. My tits quivered beneath his fingertips and I groaned when he leaned up to flick his tongue against one nipple, making me glad we had the entire night to ourselves. I wanted to feel his tongue fluttering against my clit again, but for now, his fingers sufficed.

Abandoning myself to the pleasure, I closed my eyes and rolled my hips, undulating above him. Bracing one hand against his chest, I traced the other over my own body, squeezing my breast then sliding it up to my neck and then to my mouth. I sucked on my own fingers and heard the audible hitch in Tommy's breath. The sound prompted me to open my eyes and look down at him, meeting and holding his gaze.

Being above him put his dick in the perfect spot for stimulating my g-spot. His thick cock-head rubbed against it with each thrust, strumming my pleasure and building up the mounting tension. My breathy cries began to pitch higher and higher, while his deepened.

Burying my fingernails into his chest, I involuntarily spasmed and tensed from head to toe. I threw my head back and cried out as I climaxed. My tightly drawn body released in an explosive burst. Tommy never neglected my clit, intuitively rubbing me the entire time until I clenched in a viselike grip, an orgasm that seemed to last forever until a minute later he joined me while kneading my breasts with one large hand.

Tension drained away and left me completely and utterly relaxed. I slumped down over Tommy's chest and waited for my breathing to even out.

"You're amazing." Tommy nuzzled his face into my throat and wrapped his arms tight around me. "Not gonna move now."

"Mmn, good. Stay."

Sleep dragged me under before his cock even slipped free from my body.

***

Waking up to a warm body beside me was something new and unexpected. It only took a minute to realize the fantastic dream I had was reality, and not some crazed sexual fantasy my brain had concocted.

"Morning, Em." Tommy's warm breath feathered against my ear.

Rolling over in his loose embrace brought him into my bleary vision. A few blinks cleared most of the haziness, but it was his smile that sped my heart.

"Your face looks so much better today."

"Or maybe it didn't look as bad as you thought."

I raised my fingers to his cheek and traced the splash of purple blending to green. Hadn't it been larger and fresher? "Did you really stop a robbery?"

"Yeah, up at Mabel's diner."

"Oh God, was anyone hurt?"

"Nah. Just me and the asshole sticking up the place. Trust me, you should have seen the other guy."

Despite his claims, I took care to rest my head on the unbruised side of his chest. The lazy strokes of his fingers through my hair almost put me to sleep again. "Hey Tommy, about last night…"

"Like I said, don't worry about it. I'll swing by the hardware store after work and get your water back on by tonight." The reassurance included a kiss against my brow then his blue eyes drifted to the digital clock on my nightstand. He swore under his breath and slid from beneath the sheets to pace in front of my bedroom window. A few slanted beams of sunlight highlighted his glorious body.

"Oh, okay."

The sheets pooled around my waist as I sat up. For a moment, I considered tugging them up to cover my breasts, but I wasn't ashamed. Tommy's appreciative glance roved over me as freely as mine did over his body... and his morning hard-on.

"Ah, to hell with it," Tommy muttered. "I'm going to be late as it is."

Neither of us could claim to be tired when we finally crawled out of my bed. Our morning bout of sex left me feeling energized, ready to face another dreary day waiting tables.

"I'm just going to grab some clean clothes then I'll head on over for a shower."

"If I'm gone before you get there..." He leaned in and stole a last kiss. "See you tonight to fix that pipe," he called before dashing outside in his boxers.

His promises made me as giddy as the sex between us.

"That you, Thomas?" Oh no. Someone was outside. I peeked out the window, wondering how far Tommy had gotten. Almost halfway from the looks of it.

"Morning, Mr. Davis!" I heard him call back, waving as he darted across the grass. He almost slipped once on the morning dew.

Shit. Mr. Davis was the block's biggest gossip. Our business would be across Atropos by noon, spreading quickly once he opened the barbershop for the day. I groaned into my hands.

CHAPTER 12

~CERES~

I scrutinized the werewolf in front of me. The smell of sex and sweet almond oil clung to his skin. When he hadn't come back last night, I'd assumed the job wasn't an easy fix, but I never expected to awaken to an empty bed and no man beside me.

"Well at least tell me about it."

"What?"

"Was it good? Was *she* good?"

"You want me to give you a play-by-play *now*? Baby, I have to get to work before Harrison guilt trips me about screwing off on my last days with him."

"You were due at work fifteen minutes ago," I pointed out. Our clinic was closed today, granting me time to recuperate from my cramps in peace.

"Look, if you want to know so bad, ask her when she comes over to shower." He gave me the rundown on what happened with the pipes then sprinted into the bathroom.

133

Tommy's scent was strong on the woman at the door. Emma flashed me a shy smile when I greeted her and directed her inside.

"Thanks, Ceres. Tommy had to shut off the pipes outside and I'm a mess."

A sweaty, sex rumpled, positively glowing mess.

"Sure, you can use my bathroom upstairs," I told her. Along the way, we stole peeks at each other, both too shy and uncertain to bring up last night. At least, I was. Emma waited until we were behind closed doors in my bedroom.

"I slept with Tommy last night," she blurted in a rush.

"I know."

Emotion flooded Emma's face as she doubled over with relief. "Thank God. He told me you allowed it, but I had to know he wasn't running some game on both of us. I don't know what came over me, Ceres, one moment I was planning to tell him to get the fuck out of my house and in the next we were in bed and…"

"I know," I repeated. When I stepped close, I wrapped my arms around her in a hug. "It's okay. Anything he told you, you can take as absolute truth, okay? We'll talk more after you've had your shower."

With Emma settled in to get ready, I skipped back to Tommy's room and tickled him in his ribs before he could finish buttoning his shirt. He snapped his teeth at me in return.

"How's our guest?"

"Showering and not freaking out. She fessed up to me just in case you were lying. The way she worded it though, it makes me think she felt a pull to you, too. Like she couldn't resist."

"Damnit, I wish I could stay."

"Call in," I told him. "Harrison would understand."

"I already did call in to work."

"Then what's the problem?"

Tommy stepped in front of the mirror to knot his tie. I sighed and swatted his hands away to do it for him. "You dad texted, hun. My next trial is today. I can blow off work but I can't disregard a call from the Alpha."

"Damn, he doesn't waste time. Go one then, I'll handle things here."

We kissed before he left, then I jogged up the steps to find Emma had finished her shower. She brushed out her hair before the bathroom sink with the door open to release the humid air. Seeing her in little more than a towel, my towel, sped my already racing pulse.

"Oh, hey Ceres. I'll be out of your way in a minute."

"No rush. Do you have a while to stay and eat breakfast with me, Em? And to... talk?" I asked.

"I'd like that."

Instead of preparing breakfast alone, we worked side by side. I tended the bacon and eggs while she made the fluffy pancakes. Mine always came out dense. She and I were as different as night and day, an old cliché but apt in our situation. Her bronzed skin, straight dark hair, and brown eyes contrasted my rosy glow, blonde waves, and green eyes.

"We're both crazy about you, and we've talked about this for a while since realizing it. Tommy wanted me to tell you he's sorry he didn't hang around for this chat..."

"No, it's okay. He had work and, well, I'd already made him late enough." Emma set food out on the table. "I have to admit. I never expected you to be down for that sort of thing."

"If you're not okay with it, we'll understand. I don't want you to feel pressured and he doesn't want you to feel used. Christ, I hate speaking for him." But I knew my mate's mind, his heart, and his soul on every matter now. Anxiety had dried my mouth, forcing me to wet it with a sip of OJ.

"What exactly do you want?" Emma asked.

Wild and impulsive, I kissed her without any warning and threaded my fingers through her sleek black hair. Maple syrup flavored her tongue, a sweet treat that darted shyly between my lips. Within seconds, I'd taken her response as acceptance and skimmed my fingers over her thigh.

Kissing girls never felt the same as kissing a guy. Most guys were eager to grope and feel, shoving their tongues down my throat, choking me, always going straight for the goods. Emma's kisses were unhurried, one gentle stroke past my lips after the next. Unlike Tommy, her fingers didn't immediately slide over my tits.

When our lips parted, my only regret was that it had to end. I settled back against the counter and gazed at her through heavy-lidded eyes, feeling thoroughly kissed and completely satisfied aside from the dull ache between my thighs.

"He wants you, and I want you. You like us. What's the problem here, Emma?"

"Everyone will know… this town…" She ran her fingers through her hair and sank down in a chair at the table.

"No one knows we're dating. As far as they'll know, he's moved on, he's with you, and the two of us are friends now."

"That doesn't seem fair to you, hiding what you are to him."

I've been hiding my whole life, concealing my true nature from the human world and living as a werewolf. I laughed again, amused and embittered by the irony, but unable to escape its truth. "*I* know what's fair to me. Tell me that he didn't give you the best sex you've had in all your life and I'll let this go," I blurted out. "Do something for yourself, Emma. No one has to know. It's our business."

"Tommy was great, but—"

"Tell me that you didn't like kissing me."

"I haven't kissed a woman since before Jamie was born, and..." She tugged on the ends of her hair. "This is moving too fast."

"Take all of the time you need. What I said doesn't have an expiration date. We'll wait."

~THOMAS~

If Argus called brawling with a werebear easy, then I had no illusions of the next task being anything less than deadly. I just hadn't expected it to come the day after the first one.

I sat within a high-backed, comfortable chair in Argus' office. A pretty omega girl with chestnut brown hair offered me a scotch on the rocks. Argus kept the good stuff in his liquor cabinet.

"Thanks, Nuri."

137

Her wide smile revealed teeth that were a little too sharp to pass as entirely human. After she finished serving, she shrugged off her sundress and padded to the corner where a pile of cushions awaited her. Argus' nubile assistant sprawled in her natural wolf form.

"Your only warning was to dress nicely for this. Do I get to ask what you want from me now?"

"You're to conduct a business deal," Argus replied.

"Oh. Okay. That sounds easy."

"With Saul Drakenstone, on behalf of our pack."

Some of the scotch went down the wrong pipe. I coughed until I was red in the face while Argus observed with a bemused smile on his face. "You want me to *what?*" I choked out.

"You have proven you are capable of protecting members of your pack from harm. Your strength isn't in question, Thomas. But there are times when, as Alpha, it will become necessary to broker deals between the other forces in our world."

"So you pick a dragon?" Fuck. I was playing on hard mode now. He skipped right to the top of the food chain.

Everyone in the shifter community knew about Saul Drakenstone and his household. He ran a movie studio in Los Angeles and had recently bonded to a human woman. That was another story in itself.

Argus chuckled. "As long as you don't insult him, he shouldn't eat you."

"Gee. That makes me feel so much better."

I drained my scotch for an extra dose of courage. From what I understood from past interactions, meetings with dragons were a mere courtesy. Hector and Daphne once shared stories with us about the great wyrm Ares of Greece, a dragon notorious for doing as he pleased. Most of his kind put on a show of false benevolence, but at the end of the day they took whatever they desired. The trick was to convince them that what they wanted was part of your plan.

The dragon appeared in a radiant wave of golden light and jasmine-scented smoke. A woman stood at his side dressed in silks reminiscent of the Middle East. She bowed to us and vanished in a blaze of smokeless fire. A djinn. Shit. The more I learned about the supernatural world, the scarier it became.

Shaking off my astonishment, I rose from my seat and shook his hand. "A pleasure to meet you..." Did dragons liked to be called mister?

"Saul. Call me Saul. You would be Thomas, I presume?"

I darted a look toward Argus to find him behind his desk smiling slyly. "I am, sir."

"Splendid. Let us get down to business then, shall we? A recent attack on my property has made me rethink my security measures. I feel as though a few wolves would do nicely."

A few heartbeats passed before I found my voice. "You want our omegas?"

"A proper initial wager, but my interest lies in your betas. A mere servant may be found anywhere." My stomach sank to the floor and cold swept over my body. I couldn't do that. Omegas valued food, love, and security — belonging. They would be as happy with Saul as they would among our pack as long as he treated them well. The betas were a different story.

As the Alpha, Argus frequently had to make the difficult decisions no one else wanted to make. It was like making a sacrifice to the older gods, sending off the virgin to be burnt at the pyre to save a village.

How could I do it?

"How many?" I asked quietly.

"A half dozen.

"No," my instincts blurted out.

"No?" Saul's blond brows rose. He resembled a Viking in his human form, bearing a strong resemblance to a Norse god. I tensed in the seat and waited for him to smite me for my impudence. When that didn't come, I stole a glance toward Argus from the corner of my eye. He watched me just as closely.

"Our betas have autonomy to live their lives outside of the pack. They have careers, families, and complete freedom."

Saul wasn't discouraged. "Are you not learning to become the leader of this pack? It is their duty to perform as you command."

"It's slavery," I gritted out evenly.

Argus spoke of making difficult decisions, but I couldn't have the sale of free wolves over my head.

"And what if I should take them as I choose?" Saul's eyes, as vivid as liquid gold, seemed to shine all the more brightly. His features hardened, taking on a cool appearance and losing all of the friendly demeanor.

Had Argus given me this task so he wouldn't have to do it? I had think fast on my feet.

"You seem like a reasonable man. Do you really want a guard watching over your valuables who resents you? There aren't many differences in the strength of the omegas and betas, Saul. Think about it. They understand their placement in the pack hierarchy and have no interest in human civilization.

They'll serve you faithfully." I paused, focused on maintaining a straight face as much as I was determined to appeal to his sense of dignity and respect. "As family."

"Are they not beasts in human skin? What good is a dim-witted servant to me?"

My nails bit into the palms of my hands. Fear for my fellow wolves and for myself made me cautious. Was it all an act like his werebear friend, or was the indignant fury in Saul's eyes every bit as real as it appeared?

I'd be a fool to find out. The dragon straightened in his seat, eyeballing me without humor or pity.

"With all due respect, many could say the same of your kin. Dragons first who then took human form. Our omegas may not know the full complexities of human nature, but they know loyalty. You say you're looking for guards, not diplomats."

"True, but what do your omegas have to offer me?"

He hadn't roasted me for my impudence yet, so I took it as a good sign and continued to follow my gut. Turning in my seat, I looked over to the lounging wolf across the room.

"Nuri, would you come here?"

She rose with a stretch, displaying her toned physique and shiny russet coat. A moment later she stood as a person, then bent down to pluck up her sundress and pull it on.

Saul earned my respect back when he didn't ogle Nuri like a piece of meat.

"We taught Nuri to read and write a few years ago when she first joined our pack," I explained. "The same is true for all of our omegas. She's intelligent, hardworking, and as loyal as any beta. She's worth a dozen of us, but she has no family and no mortal life among humans. She never complains and always pulls her share of the work. And since she's served Argus personally, she's trained in maintaining an office."

"That does make her quite valuable indeed."

"Thomas," Nuri started to protest. Color rose high in her cheeks and spread across her skin.

"It's true," I insisted. "Would you like to go with him?"

Nuri hesitated. Her large eyes drifted to Argus and sought his approval. He shook his head gently.

"I have no bearing on this negotiation," Argus spoke up. "This is between you, Thomas, and Saul."

"Then I go with him. It will be my honor," she said, giving no hesitation.

Saul stroked his beard thoughtfully. "Ahh… she is but one, and I came in search of six."

"And given her worth and value, I believe you've received the better end of the bargain, Saul," I said, hoping to trick him at his own game.

His cool stare turned my blood to ice, sending a chill down my spine. I suppressed the urge to shiver and watched him finally turn in his seat to face Nuri. "Tell me what you think of this, little one."

"I like to help people," Nuri said kindly. "What duties will I have?"

"Protection of something far more valuable to me than anything found in my hoard." He paused and seemed to study Nuri. "How do you like children?"

Nuri smiled brightly. While her aspirations, hopes, and plans for the future were simple, they were no indication of her intelligence. "I love them. I have cared for many pups. I find human children as enjoyable. Will I get to play with many?"

Her enthusiasm was infectious, bringing a smile to Saul's face as well. "Only one," he replied.

"I'll allow you to have her under two conditions, Saul." With some focus, I continued to take measured and even breaths, hoping to conceal that I was freaking out on the inside the entire time. "On your honor as a dragon."

"Oh?" Again, his brows rose.

"You have to give her time to say goodbye to her friends, and you'll treat her as a member of your household, not a servant. She must be family."

"A reasonable request." He turned his head toward Argus and grinned. "I think this one has potential. Now, if you'll both excuse me, I will inform my mate of our new house member and send Mahasti for Nuri tomorrow at noon, if that suits you." He looked back at me for confirmation.

It took me a moment to find my voice. "She'll be ready."

"Excellent."

We shook hands, signed a formal contract detailing the arrangement, and then Saul called upon his djinn to return home. Once the floral mist dissipated, I sunk down in my seat and reached for the remainder of my whiskey. "Argus... was that real?"

"You handled that well, son. Quick thinking," Argus said.

"That's not what I asked. Was. That. Real?" I repeated, enunciating each word and staring at him from across the desk.

"Jason failed and he's still here, if that's what you're asking. He insulted Saul and gave away half of our betas to soothe the damage and complete brokering the deal." Argus shook his head, his lip curling with disgust. "After Saul made Jason piddle like a bad puppy, I dismissed him from the room and the two of us had a good laugh at his expense."

"Holy shit. Does Jason know it wasn't real?"

Argus chuckled and refilled my glass himself. "No. Let's keep it that way and let him think I fixed it all in his absence. If we told him no, Saul would have gone to ask another pack for a volunteer. He's not like other dragons."

I understood now why he wouldn't share any information about Jason's trial with Ceres and me. Shuddering, I managed to suppress the terror that lingered in the wake of Saul's departure.

"Do you think Nuri will be happy with him?"

The Alpha's sad smile revealed the identity of the lover Ceres saw leaving his room. "He's a good man, and you made the choice I would have made in your place. The choice I hoped you would make, at least."

"I'm sorry, Argus."

"I'm sorry to see her go, but she'll be happier there. It was time."

We sat in silence, sipping our drinks. The quiet gave me the time to steady my nerves after the meeting, but it also brought to mind a ton of questions I'd been considering the past couple of weeks. Having Argus alone became the perfect opportunity to discover more about what becoming the Alpha meant for my future.

"You did well, Thomas. Take a measure of confidence from what you did here today, but don't let it make you cocky. You have one trial left, but for now, go celebrate with your friends. I know a certain raven who would love to hear about your first-hand encounter with a dragon."

Harrison would never let me live it down if he found out what happened through another source. Besides, time out with the guys sounded like a great plan after all my women issues.

"Thanks, Argus. I'll see you at the next pack gathering."

CHAPTER 13

ONE MONTH LATER

~EMMA~

I spied a pair of wolves in my backyard early one morning. The unusual sighting sent me running for the camera, but by the time I found it, the two magnificent animals were gone.

That evening, one appeared again and approached my son. I was stacking plates from the dishwasher when I heard Jamie's excited, "Mom! Mom!" from the back yard.

Wolves held a place of honor among the Potawatomi, but mother's instinct drove me outside onto the patio to protect my son. My worries were unfounded, because the placid dark-furred wolf only licked Jamie's fingers and nuzzled his chest. When I approached, he sat on his haunches and placed his forepaws on my thigh, displaying behavior I'd never witnessed in any wild animal.

Jamie spent the entire night on the phone with both sets of grandparents. He couldn't wait to tell them about his encounter. A week later, I almost had to force my boy away for his annual visit to Dallas with his paternal grandparents. He wanted to see his wolf again and… so did I.

I didn't know what to do with myself during the lonely interim period. Tommy and Ceres had other ideas. My days were divided between working extra hours and practically living next door.

Ceres was waiting on my stoop when I pulled in the driveway at the end of my seventh work day. She bounded to her feet and flung her arms around me the moment I was out of my car.

"Emma, I have the best idea and I need your help."

"Tell me inside, my feet are killing me."

In less than five minutes we were settled on the couch with cold glasses of sangria. When I wiggled my aching toes, Ceres pulled my feet into her lap without prompting. I reciprocated, and with our legs weaved together, we delivered mutual massages while the television droned the evening news. She knew exactly where to press her fingers.

"You're so much better at this than Tommy."

After her case of giggles ended, Ceres nodded in agreement. "His back massages put me to sleep, but feet? Pfft."

"He always ends up tickling me instead. So what's this big idea of yours?"

147

"A surprise birthday party for Tommy this weekend." Ceres' eyes shone with her excitement, the emerald color brighter than I remembered.

"Yeah? Did you have thoughts for it?"

"I was thinking we could decorate upstairs, bake a cake, and just pamper him."

"I'm gonna go out on a limb here and guess he's not much for celebrating his birthday."

"Bingo. And… he hasn't been since his mom died on her way here to visit him for his 19th birthday party."

I winced. "I can't really blame him then."

"Yeah. So I had this crazy idea to give him new birthday memories. Sucks that Jamie's gone until the end of summer, but we can just…" Ceres flailed with a hand, searching for the words to say.

"Copious amounts of booze and his favorite tit and gore movies?" I suggested.

"Yep."

"I'm in. I have a shift Friday morning but the rest of the weekend off. That'll give me plenty of time to frost a cake and help you get things ready."

Ceres squeezed my foot and grinned. "It'll be so much fun."

With our heads together, we perfected our devilish plan. An outing to the store the next day allowed us to rummage through the bargain DVD bin, where we found a bounty of Tommy's favorites. His new job had stolen most of our time together recently, bringing Ceres and I together more than ever.

"Don't forget the Reese's Cups. He loves those," I reminded Ceres as we passed the snack bin.

"If he eats all of that *and* a cake, his teeth are going to rot out of his mouth," she mumbled.

"I think we all deserve one night of chocolate overindulgence."

"All right, but don't say I didn't warn you. He gets really horny when he's hyper."

I circled my thumb over Ceres' inner wrist and tugged her toward the checkout line. Our cartload of goodies ensured we had everything needed for one hell of a celebration.

"So, where's Tommy tonight?" I asked on our way to the car.

"He had an emergency service call out in San Antonio. He's repairing servers and stuff now, I think, and somebody wanted their shit up tonight."

"Do you want to hang over at my place then?" I bit my lower lip and watched her as I shut the trunk. Her green eyes flicked between me and the car, rife with indecision.

"Oh no... Not tonight. I told Dad I'd come over after I finished shopping. Him and my mom split, so he's been real lonely over there by himself."

Ceres climbed into the passenger side and belted herself in. After I rounded the car to the driver's side, I found a flyer tucked beneath my wiper. The smug face of her ex-boyfriend smiled up at me along with a hotline number and request for any info. I crumpled it up, afraid she'd get upset if I showed her.

"Oh crap, I'm sorry to hear that. I remember you mentioning problems but I had no idea," I said. When she wasn't looking, I tossed the wadded up paper on the floor in the back seat.

"It's been a long time coming. Dad deserves better. I... I love my mom, but I don't love the things she does to him. To both of us." Ceres sighed and leaned back against the headrest, her eyes half-lidded, thoughtful in the dwindling light. "Sometimes I wonder if watching them is what ruined traditional relationships for me."

"You and your dad sound pretty close. And I think, maybe, you just didn't know what you were looking for before."

"He's pretty open with me. She told him she was done with him, and if he ever wanted to have sex again he'd better get a lover because she planned to have one of her own." She chuckled, quiet and bitter laughter. "I couldn't imagine saying that to Tommy, but I guess it's different when you actually love someone."

"Hey, Ceres?" I stole a glance at the woman in my passenger seat, her short skirt higher than mid-thigh. "Why me? What do both of you get out of inviting me into your relationship?"

"Because I can't get you off of my mind, Emma, and Tommy feels the same way. There's not a day that we're together that I don't think about having my hands all over you. And I don't just want to fuck you, I want to watch Tommy do it. I want to be there to whisper in your ear after I tell him to stick you with his cock. I want to make you come with my fingers while I suck him off."

My mouth became dry and my heart skipped a beat. Her words touched me, painting an intimate portrait of the ideas that had been skimming my mind since our tentative dating began. "I want the same thing, too."

Drawn to her, I leaned over the center console and hugged her, then pressed a kiss to her cheek. A second kiss followed, a nibble at the corner of her mouth, then a playful suckle against her bottom lip. What I'd meant as an act of comfort turned into an insatiable need to be closer. A hungry groan parted her lips.

As our kiss deepened, my hands wandered in shameless exploration. Ceres only wore a camisole beneath her scoop neck tank, no bra to contain her small breasts. I imagined rosy pink nipples beneath it, and a tweak from my fingers stiffened one to a hard, pebbled tip.

Ceres' fingers slipped under my jeans waistband. I cursed the snug fit when she couldn't wriggle her hand down far enough to ease the growing ache between my thighs. The memory of her words taunted me, but in my fantasy our roles were reversed. I wanted to be the one who made her writhe and come, using my tongue instead of my fingers.

Shopping buggies banged together. I jerked away from her and cracked my elbow against the door, then scanned the immediate area. A store employee pushed a dozen carts past the rear of my vehicle.

"Scared the shit out of me," Ceres muttered.

"Me, too. Uh. Not that there's… anything to be ashamed about."

A rosy flush covered her cheeks. Mine burned hot, too, and no matter how much I wanted to resume, I started the car and reversed from the parking spot. We cruised onto the road and set on our journey home.

"Emma? Do you believe in soulmates?" Ceres asked.

"I believe in fate, but I don't know about soulmates. It sounds a little too much like a fairy tale to me. Why?"

"Don't you think our meeting is more than coincidence? Of all the people to rent the house beside us, it had to be you."

Three deer bounded across the road ahead of us. They cleared safely and I let out my pent up breath. "Wow, that was clo—"

"Look out!"

A fourth deer — larger than the others with an impressive antler rack — leapt from the bushes. I slammed on the brakes and tried to swerve into the vacant lane. It was no use. The deer crashed into my front fender and crumpled my car. Momentum carried us forward until the deer's heavy body rolled over the hood and smashed against my windshield. It cracked beneath the buck's weight, sending glass splinters into the car.

~THOMAS~

"What's taking Ceres so long to get here?" Argus demanded.

I glanced down at my phone and the five unanswered text messages. My attempt to call Emma and ask her to pop over failed when our neighbor didn't answer her home line either. Were they out together? Were they okay?

Vesta came unglued when the scheduled time came and passed without her daughter present. "It's of no surprise to any of us that Ceres fails to acknowledge the profound importance of this trial. Such disrespect for our practices."

The rest of my patience vanished. "You're just pissed she isn't here to see your pet lose to me."

"Why you impertinent pu—"

"We should wait," Argus interrupted his wife. "Try calling her again, Thomas."

"Stalling won't change the outcome, Argus," Vesta snapped. "You set the time. Honor it or continue to look weak in front of the pack."

"Jason has already lost one trial." The corner of Argus' mouth rose. "Are you so eager for him to lose another?"

"It's fine, Argus. Let's go. I'm ready to kick his ass and get this over with."

I stripped out of my clothes while the rest of our pack gathered and watched the property edge with interested eyes. Vesta took Jason's clothes as he passed them off. I'd never pitied Argus before, but I'd never forget the hurt in his eyes, and I'd never forgive Vesta for changing from the den mother I once loved like my own.

"The first to discover the hidden animal, slay it, and return will win the third and final trial."

"What do I need to find?" Jason asked.

Argus extended black velvet sack toward us. "Since you're in the lead, you get to draw, Thomas."

I plucked a sheet of paper from it blindly and unfolded it. *Shit!* Something told me Vesta had been the malicious soul who picked the targets. Why Argus had agreed… well, there was no telling.

"Badger," I read out loud. I inhaled the smell on the paper then passed it to my opponent.

"Afraid, Weston?" Jason smirked.

"Afraid for your pretty face." Badgers were notorious fighters and vicious little bastards.

I shifted, contorting my bones and adopting my wolf body. With my nose raised to the air, I sniffed and searched for the scent.

In a property spanning hundreds of acres, my goal could be anywhere on Argus and Vesta's land. At the signal, we raced as fast as our legs would carry us, traveling on fleet paws across the grass into wilder, unkempt ground. Jason's bulk and muscle slowed him down and put me in the lead. I broke into the forest first and charged without stopping.

Badger. Knowing Argus and Vesta, there would only be one. It could be anywhere, its scent marked in numerous places to throw us off the track.

Even Vesta wouldn't risk dishonoring herself by giving Jason the upper hand. I cleared that thought from my mind and continued forward at a jog. I kept my eyes open and my ears raised, searching beneath the light of the full moon for my opponent.

Seconds turned to minutes and minutes became an hour beneath the full moon. I ran a perimeter and tightened it with every lap until I picked up a whiff of my prey.

Bingo, I thought. With my nose to guide me, I raced forward at full speed. With a hint of Jason's scent in the air, I knew it was only a matter of time before one of us reached the goal. I had to beat him to it.

My only warning was a deep, rumbling growl. The cougar was upwind of me and I hadn't smelled her coming until it was too late. She dived from her higher perch, throwing her muscled bulk between me and my prey. The badger was already dead, its bloody carcass lying on the top of the slope.

Fuck my life.

I tried to lunge to the side, but the cougar swatted at me and caught my shoulder. She ripped through my fur and into the flesh beneath. The mountain lion had fifty pounds on me at least, her large body composed of the heavy muscle my lean frame lacked. Her hiss might as well have come from the bowels of hell

As she stood between me and my target, Jason sprang into view at the top of the hill. Shameless as ever, the bastard claimed the dead badger in his teeth and ran for it. He loped away on all four paws while the cougar boxed me in. I stepped to the side and sought my escape route as the cat advanced on me.

~CERES~

Emma and I both screamed until the vehicle stopped an eternity later. By the end, the stag's flailing hoof was inches from Emma's terrified face, but the injured animal was trapped on the dash. For a few seconds, the only sounds filling the car were our panicked, hyperventilating breaths and his dying grunts.

My neck hurt, but it wouldn't take long for the pain to fade. I healed faster than Thomas; a natural born werewolf with sharper, more attuned talents. "Are you all right?"

"A little shaken up but not hurt, I think. You?"

"A couple cuts but nothing big," I answered.

We spilled out of the car and walked around the front end to survey the damage. The buck's body lay on the hood, twisted at an impossible angle, but he continued to take labored breaths and occasionally kick at the damaged windshield.

"It's suffering," Emma murmured sadly. "God, he came out of nowhere."

"It wasn't your fault. It just happens sometimes on these roads," I consoled her. "I better call Dad and let him know I'll… Oh no. Oh no, oh no!" I whipped my phone out of my pocket and glanced down at the time. I had less than an hour to reach the pack meeting for his final trial and we weren't even in a service area. "I forgot this road has no signal!"

"What should we do then? Wait for someone to come by?" Emma pulled out her older model clamshell phone. It slipped from her shaking hands and clattered on the asphalt. "Fuck!"

"Emma, sweetie, it's okay."

"I've never been in an accident before," she admitted. "I can't afford for them to total out my car either." With my arms around her, the shakes diminished and she relaxed. I ran my fingers through her hair and kissed her brow.

"Here. We're going to turn the emergency lights on. I want you to stay over here between the passenger side and the road while I go for help." I guided her to safety alongside the road.

"Help?"

"Thomas has a friend who lives two miles down this road. I can make it." I tossed my heels into the open driver's side.

"Two miles is kind of a long way in the dark like this, Ceres… Is it safe?"

"I ran track in school. I'll be fine. There's nothing out here but whitetails like our friend there."

It could be an hour or more before some motorist came along on this road, and I couldn't wait that long when Harrison lived nearby. I started running, holding my phone in one hand.

Once I was out of her sight and around the bend, I stepped off the road into the bushes. I hung my leggings, shirt, and panties on a tree branch then shifted for a run through the wilderness with my cellphone in my mouth.

My howl brought Harrison outside for me to assume my human form and relay the news to him. He brought his truck in a hurry, allowing me to nab my clothes where I left them.

"She's going to wonder how the hell you got to me and back so fast."

"So? We'll tell her that I flagged you down in passing. You were on your way out for beer or something."

Emma swallowed the story we fed her, and less than fifteen minutes later Harrison had hitched her vehicle and begun towing it home. He put the stag down, using the pistol he kept in his truck. Emma shot us both grossed out looks when we dragged the beast into the bed of the truck.

"What? Waste not, want not," Harrison said.

The quick drive ended when we pulled in front of her house. We could have walked it in the dark, but then I would have never made it to Thomas' trial in a timely manner and Emma's old Chevy would still need a tow.

"You sure you're going to be okay, Emma?"

"Yeah. The insurance folk will be out in the morning and I called work to tell the night manager I won't be there in the morning."

"Get some rest."

Harrison received a show when Emma and I kissed goodnight. She was too shaken for me to allow the opportunity to pass without affection. Smart bird that he was, he kept his mouth shut about it and unhooked her car.

The moment we pulled back out onto the road I yanked my phone from my purse. "Dad?"

"Ceres, where are you? The trial just began."

"I got into a wreck — I'm not hurt," I quickly blurted out. "I wanted to let you know I'll be late."

Dad breathed a relieved exhale into the phone. "Get here when you can then."

"I will. Harrison's driving so we'll be there soon."

We were there in record time to find most of the pack sitting vigil in the rear yard. Garden torches burned, illuminating the estate's majestic patio. Dad sat alone with a glass in his hand — he hadn't been the same since Nuri left. My heart ached for him.

"Ah, there you are," my father greeted me when I crossed his field of vision.

I dropped into the seat beside him. "How long has it been since they left?"

"Two hours, give or take. I thought we'd see Thomas by now. Hell, we killed it and placed it on the ridge. Had all of the omegas take turns touching it to every tree they could find."

"Jesus, dad, that's going to attract all sorts of scavengers looking for a free meal."

Dad sipped his bourbon and chuckled. "So it will. Otherwise, it wouldn't be much of a challenge. So how bad was the wreck? Anyone hurt?" He glanced at me again, scanning for visible bumps and bruises, no doubt.

"We were both okay. A little shook up. I hate leaving her alone after that but I couldn't not be here for Tommy." My worries were torn between the two, so I passed the time waiting for Tommy by texting Emma to make sure she was fine.

Our planning stage continued until I saw the black silhouette of a wolf in the distance, racing across the grass.

"I see one of them!" Daphne cried.

"Is it Thomas?" Hector asked.

I squinted. The figure was bulky, too broad at the shoulder and flank. Too tall. Too slow. Not my Thomas.

"Shit," Dad muttered under his breath. For the sake of neutrality, he wore an even expression when Jason arrived to drop his quarry. He shifted to his human body and wiped his mouth with the back of a hand.

"I win, right?"

"You've succeeded. Congratulations, Jason."

Dad excused himself and walked away to send out the signal to Thomas. His howl toward the forest edge — meant to announce the end of the hunt — ran a shiver up my spine. Only the oldest wolves could pull off a perfect howl in their human skin.

Vesta couldn't contain her smile. It hurt to see her beaming at Jason instead of my father, but I couldn't hate her. Not really. What her wolf saw in Jason's was a mystery, but denying a fated mate was akin to ripping a limb off. It left a hole.

I hope Dad finds the wolf he deserves.

Another wolf appeared at the edge of the forest. Relieved sighs seemed to exhale from all of us.

"He's limping!" Daphne called.

I rushed across the grass barefoot, and when I reached him he transformed to his human half. Clotted blood stained his shoulder from in a triplicate series of slashes. "Oh my God, what happened to you?"

"A mountain lion," he rasped. "Fuck, this hurts."

"Somebody bring us some water!"

After we forced some fluids into Tommy, I led my mate inside to my old bedroom and let him tell his tale.

"Ugh, they should have known better than to drag a bloody carcass all over the place."

"I hate cats," Tommy groaned. He swore the whole while I cleaned his wounds, and once I medicated him, he passed out fast asleep in my bed.

And my mother claimed I wasn't a real doctor.

CHAPTER 14

~CERES~

Tommy sulked most of the next day about his loss to Jason. I kept him in bed until my dad drove us home in the evening.

As for his birthday, there was one flaw to our carefully laid out plans. Tommy's pals hijacked him for a boys' night out when he returned from work. One moment, I was stepping onto the porch to greet him with a happy birthday, and in the next, five of his closest guy pals came streaking across the yard to ambush him.

Bobby jingled his car keys and pointed back to their party van, a gross looking SUV with doors that didn't match the rest of the body's paint job. The fender was hanging off and almost dragging the ground, a casualty of the last wreck he'd gotten into that didn't total out his piece of crap.

"Oh come on guys, I wanted to hog him tonight," I whined.

"Sorry, toots." Darrell grinned at me and made a kissy face. "We've had this planned out for weeks, but I promise we'll get him home in one piece."

"Nine o'clock," I ordered.

They laughed. Even Tommy chuckled at my expense, and he was the one being spirited away. Fuck. *I* could have taken him to a party to get drunk. They'd probably take him to some gross strip club where bitches rubbed their crusty crotches in his face. I glowered at them.

"Ten?" I bartered.

"Not making promises," Harrison replied.

"I'll hook you up with my blonde friend from school," I offered the raven, dangling the possibility like bait in front of a grouper.

He perked up fast. "Your chances have dramatically increased."

Poor Tommy looked like I'd betrayed him as they took him away in their party van.

By ten o'clock, we still hadn't seen any sign of our birthday boy or heard from him on the phone. Stupid Harrison. No fucking way I was hooking his ass up now. Any of them for that matter. They'd wrecked all our careful plans.

So Emma and I made the best out of it. We enjoyed dinner but left the cake alone. That was Tommy's, even if he was late. Impromptu sugar cookies and margaritas satisfied our sweet craving.

"So," Emma began, bouncing in her seat and turning to face me. "I don't know if this is off limits or not but I'm dying to know — Does Tommy, um, growl at you in bed sometimes?"

Crap! "I think he, ah, gets really into the moment."

"I mean, I'm not complaining. It's different is all. And kind of cute. I noticed he only does it when we've been at it for a while. Where does he get the stamina?"

We both laughed after that. "I wish I knew. Does he do that thing where he wakes you up an hour after you've fallen asleep?"

"And gives you the puppy dog eyes while practically humping your leg?" Emma asked?

"Yes!"

"Oh! Oh! And does he hog the water in the shower from you too?"

"Oh my God, yes. I'll be standing there shivering because he wants to be under the spray the whole time," I complained.

So we filled more of our time with gossiping about the man of the evening while waiting for the boys to eventually return him to our care. I still wanted to cuss Harrison out for keeping him away all night, but I assuaged my hurt feelings by sharing embarrassing stories from Tommy's youth. Emma laughed so hard that she spilled her fifth or sixth margarita on her lap and leapt up screaming about the cold booze soaking into her skirt.

"Whoops! That's all right! We can fix it! It's jammy time anyway, right?"

"I'll run home—"

"Nah, don't do that. Throw on one of Tommy's shirts while I toss this in the wash."

~Thomas~

"Dude, it's just one trial. You'll kick that motherfuckah's ass and be a four-legged king by next week," Bobby said. He was behind the wheel, tasked as our designated driver for the night.

"I know, but shit, that should have been an easy win. Tracking is the one thing I do *good* as a wolf. Argus called me a natural at it when I was a kid."

Harrison rubbed his chin. "You don't think Vesta would cheat, do you?"

"A cougar side-swiped me when I went in for it, man. It was just bad luck. Jason saw his opportunity and took it."

Jameson lit another cigarette and blew his smoke out the window. "How do you know it wasn't another shifter like you?"

"I would have smelled her human half on her pelt," I explained. "Whenever we shift, our human scent remains on our fur."

"I dunno, dude. The way you talk about wolf territory and shit I'd expect their personal hunting grounds to be predator free." Bobby scratched his head and looked unconvinced.

"Animals don't have that same sense. Wolf territory among shifters is different. We can talk like humans and lay boundaries. Argus meets with the leaders of the other clans to sell and barter for ground where we can spread. Now if a wild cougar decides to come down from the hills or the surrounding wilderness, it could give a damn if there's wolves around."

"I saw a video once on YouTube of a cougar snapping a wolf's neck," Jameson commented. "Brutal."

"Case in point," I replied. "I'm lucky to be alive. Am I pissed I lost? Yeah, because I don't know if I can take him in a fight."

"That big bitch has muscles on his muscles," Bobby mused. "Bet he's slower than you."

"Anyway, you have a couple days to take it easy right? Go home, fuck one of your girls, and try to unwind until it's time," Jameson said.

"Lucky bastard," Harrison muttered.

Bobby parked in the drive. The lights upstairs were dim, illuminated by the hazy pale blue light of the television. Ceres must have been in our hangout room. I expected to find her sprawled on the couch fast asleep.

"Night guys." I waved goodbye to my pals and unlocked the door. "Ceres?" I called as I stepped inside. A line of colorful, half-melted candles greeted me, glowing from shelves and counter spaces in a trail leading to the second level.

A handmade banner dangled in my favorite colors; the blue and silver construction paper cheerfully pronounced me to be a big boy. My two favorite girls waited for me on the sofa with their long legs twined and feet placed in each other's laps.

"Uh... hi." My gaze traveled over both of them. Bottles of nail polish sat on the coffee table along with an assortment of other manicure items.

"We gave up on your birthday party and decided to make it a girls' pajama party instead," Ceres giggled.

165

Ceres wore her usual camisole and boy short ensemble. Emma had on one of my t-shirts without a bra beneath. It was snug around her big breasts.

"I didn't know you planned to do this…. Why didn't you call me?" I rubbed my face with one hand. "You didn't have to do this for me, you know."

"That would have ruined the surprise," Ceres explained. "Anyway, Happy Birthday. I did this because I love you." She threw her arms around me and Emma kissed me over her shoulder.

"Because we care and your birthday is worth celebrating."

"We ate your dinner but there's still a cake," Ceres said.

She gestured to the triple-layered confection on the table. I recognized Emma's touch in the perfectly smoothed white buttercream and neatly fanned strawberry slices. Her tidy handwriting wished me a "Happy 28th Birthday" in red icing.

Ceres slipped a DVD into the player while Emma served me cake.

"Oh, sweet! You remembered I wanted to see this!"

"Yeah, you were so busy when it was in the theater that you missed the chance."

With a sexy woman on either side of me, we enjoyed an action-packed crime thriller. At the end, when the credits rolled and a popular rock song blasted from our home theater speakers, Ceres rose from her seat and crooked her finger at Emma. The girls moved to the middle of the room between the television and coffee table, away from the food and drinks. Emma swayed and twisted to the music, possessing the grace of a sorority girl who had downed a fifth of vodka.

I leaned back with a grin on my face and enjoyed the show. "You know what would really be great? A striptease," I joked. Wishful thinking on my part.

The camisole came off first, dragged upward and over Ceres' head to bare her breasts. Both budded into stiff peaks beneath Emma's icy fingers. Her knees bent and her hands continued their downwards path. They took Ceres' white lace boy shorts down with them and completely exposed the rest of her body. As usual, she didn't wear panties.

If I were in the company of any other women, I might have reconsidered my next step, but Emma and Ceres had seen it all before. My cock ached, prompting me to free it from my jeans to hold it in one hand. I pumped a few times, watching eagerly as the girls danced and spun on the floor.

Ceres tangled her hands in Emma's black hair and cried out with surprised pleasure. It took me a minute to understand why; my gaze had been on Emma's panty-clad ass.

Emma kneeled in front of Ceres, her hands on the other girl's thighs. Her tongue curled against my mate's bald pussy and circled her clit, earning a genuine moan and cry for more. They ended up on the floor where the act continued for my eager enjoyment. My fingers slid up and down my own cock while my eyes remained fastened to the main event. Emma had sprawled on her belly to finger Ceres and divide her glistening folds with skilled tongue strokes.

"Oh shit... oh God!" Ceres' legs trembled.

And just like that, I witnessed her orgasm as a spectator rather than a participant. Emma laid a trail of kisses up the other woman's thigh to her hip, then turned her sultry gaze on me. She dumped her top on the floor next to Ceres' pile of discarded garments. Ignoring me for the moment, the two girls lay together on the floor, their firm breasts pressed close together, legs entwined.

I had two very naked, very beautiful women touching and kissing on one another. I would have given my soul to fuck them both.

As if reading my mind, they broke apart and joined me at the couch. Ceres crawled to my feet and pulled off my socks while Emma waited alongside me to pull me to my feet. Together they stripped me bare.

It had to be a dream.

It was too perfect to be anything but a dream. Hell, I wouldn't be surprised if I was lying face down on the bar top while the guys drew cocks and balls on my face with a Sharpie. I had myself convinced that this wasn't reality.

Emma kissed me with the flavor of alcohol and Ceres' snatch lingering on her lips. The combined taste made my cock jerk by reflex, a reminder of how much I loved to go down on my girls.

While I tongue wrestled Emma, Ceres deep-throated my dick. I broke for a breath and the girls swapped places, subjecting me to a sexual torment beyond anything I ever experienced. Ceres sucked my tongue into her mouth and Emma paid loving attention to my balls. Eventually, our threesome became a drunken haze of wet pussy and jiggling breasts. I lost track of whose tits ended up in my mouth and whose snatch accepted my fingers.

Ceres nudged me to a seat on the floor then held out her hand for Emma. They shared another sensual kiss then moved apart to continue whatever plans they had for me.

With my back against the couch and my head on the cushions, I became the perfect seat for Emma to straddle. She rode my face eagerly while gripping the back of the sofa. She rocked on her toes, grinding her snatch against my face. I parted her labia with my tongue and trailed the slick crease until I found her clit. I shamelessly plunged into her hole to tongue fuck her while she pretended to be the world's sexiest cowgirl.

"Tommy!" Emma cried out. "Yes, yes… just like that, baby. Fuck I love your tongue."

Ceres claimed the prime property on my lap. With Emma on my face I couldn't see the blonde, but my hands made up for my lack of sight. Her puckered nipples were at my mercy.

I couldn't say much, my mouth greedily occupied with Emma's delectable pussy. I took Ceres' hands and guided them to Emma's generous ass. Together we kneaded the soft flesh until I was certain Ceres would keep it up on her own. Managing to snake one hand up between Emma's spread legs, I discovered her grabbing her own tit.

I gobbled Emma's wet pussy, fucking her with my tongue while bucking my hips up to make sure Ceres received my every inch. Next time, I planned to take one of them from behind while watching the other get eaten out by the first. Or maybe I'd claim Ceres' ass and let the girls 69 one another.

"Oh god, oh god. I'm gonna come, Tommy. So fucking close!"

She jerked atop me and groaned in a wanton display until I flicked my tongue across her swollen clit. Emma screamed my name out in pleasure and orgasmed.

I broke the seal of my mouth with a wet pop to allow Emma to shakily flop off. Before she could move far I caught her arm and dragged her to down me for a kiss, her juices still on my tongue.

Ceres leaned forward and stole possession of Emma's mouth. Then she kissed me. Our tongues met in an awkward but immensely arousing three-person kiss that gradually became more coordinated with each passing second.

I surrendered first and let my head fall back against the couch cushions, so close to climax that I had begun to pound Ceres' pussy like a drum. I hammered her harder and faster as she cried out and clutched her fingers into my shoulders. My mate screamed first with the arrival of her orgasm, and I rode her through it without stopping, without acknowledging that her pussy contracted around my hard prick. Every thrust was one step closer to reaching my own climax.

"Fuck I'm so close," I groaned. Her pussy clenched around me, so exquisitely tight.

"C'mon, baby. Faster. Fucking ride me, Ceres," I ordered. Emma kneeled beside us and tangled her hands in Ceres' hair. They kissed.

"Fuck, you two are so hot kissing like that."

My balls drew against my body, tightening with the arrival of my orgasm. I exploded, one hot pulse after another, groaning out loud and holding her hips with bruising force. After I finished, Ceres finally climbed off me. My half-hard dick glistened with our combined juices. I was trapped somewhere between awareness and oblivion when Emma leaned down and fluttered her tongue against my cock. Ceres joined her and the women finished cleaning it off together.

Holy. Shit.

"Happy Birthday, Tommy," they both told me between worshipful and affectionate kisses.

The reality of a threesome was far more exhausting than I had anticipated. We couldn't fit together on the sofa, and the uncomfortable hardwood floor discouraged us from sprawling in front of it.

I scrubbed my hands and face like a zombie in Ceres' bathroom, and made myself guzzle a glass of water to stave off the morning hangover. Somehow we made it to the bed and curled up together with our naked bodies pressed close.

Ceres slid one leg over my thigh. Emma mirrored her from the opposite side and slipped an arm across my chest. I lay there for minutes longer listening to their deep and even breaths until at last, the world around me dimmed and I joined my beauties in sleep.

CHAPTER 15

~EMMA~

"Mm…" I stretched in bed alongside a warm body. Thomas sprawled beside me, trapped with Ceres tangled on his other side. Tracing my fingers down his body, I followed hard lines of muscular definition before stealing a peek at Ceres. The sheets had fallen below her waist.

She was beautiful, and all mine. All ours. We belonged to each other.

"Morning, Em," Ceres muttered. She yawned and propped her body onto one elbow. "Tommy is always last to wake up after a night of drinking."

"He looks so peaceful now." I stroked her fingers over Tommy's dark hair.

"Should we make breakfast?"

"I'll do it. I've already tasted your pancakes, remember?"

Ceres stuck her tongue out at me.

"They're like flour bricks," Tommy mumbled. Our drowsy lover raised his head and glanced back at me. "Don't ever let her into the kitchen for breakfast unless it's French toast and eggs," he warned.

"Ass."

I laughed at the two of them and hugged my body to his muscular back. When I placed my arm around him and slid my fingers down his abs, I found his cock rigid and ready beneath the sheets.

As if she sensed my intentions, Ceres leaned over him to claim my mouth, a sweet kiss on the borderline between tender and hungry. I starved for her, too.

"Where's your vibrator, Ceres?" Tommy asked.

"In the drawer. Why?"

Tommy had something in mind. After he propped the pillows up behind him, he sprawled on his back with his big cock standing tall. I tucked my hair behind my ear and leaned down to swirl my tongue around the tip. Ceres sealed her lips at the base.

"Here, baby, lie on your back on me." Tommy tugged Ceres down. "Emma, how'd you like to fuck us both?"

It took me all of two seconds to understand what Tommy wanted as he passed me a glittery purple dildo. I straddled his hips and sank down over his thick cock. He stretched my snatch for the perfect fit while Ceres watched, her spread thighs offering me open access to her baby smooth pussy. I thumbed on the vibrator then slid the sex toy inside her body.

Undulating my hips, I rode Tommy and used each rocking motion to slide the vibrator in and out. Ceres moaned.

Another soft hum added to the noise in the room. Tommy had chosen the mini-vibe designed to cover a finger like a thimble. The studded surface on the finger pad had a powerful vibration that he teased over my left breast. Each skim past my tight nipple was torture.

Ceres' body twisted atop Tommy as I angled the vibrating silicone tips against her clit while I worked the rest of the dildo in quick rocks.

"Damn, it's sexy watching you two," he gritted out.

"Fuck yes, Emma, fuck. I'm so close," Ceres cried. Her eyes shut and mouth opened wide, a shudder going through her tensed body. Tommy and I watched her climax then I tossed the toy aside on the bed and squeezed her breasts. My thighs quivered with exertion, my breaths quickened, and my heartbeat pounded loudly in my head.

"I need you deeper, Tommy," I gasped. "Please, I can't... I need..." I couldn't find the words to express the sudden yearning I had for him. For them both.

"Move," he groaned. Ceres scrambled off, and before I could move, Tommy had bumped me off of his hips. He planted me face down amidst the rumpled sheets and grabbed two handfuls of my ass. His cock split me again in the new position, hammering me with hard and fast thrusts. I knew he was close, a wild animal behind me. His low growl clenched my pussy in anticipation, and then I was coming with him as he spurted his load.

"Mine, Em. *Mine*," he groaned against my shoulder. He nipped me with his teeth. "Be mine."

"I *am* yours."

He slammed forward again, grinding against me with nowhere to go. The tip of his dick struck my cervix and his balls clapped against my clit. Tommy's movement set off a chain reaction and lit through my soul, igniting in a brilliant rush of ecstasy. My pussy spasmed around his cock in a surprising second orgasm. Ceres twisted onto her side to kiss me, muffling my cries.

I couldn't take anymore. It was too much. Too intense. A molten explosion tore through my body and shook my limbs until I was paralyzed with pleasure.

"Tommy!" I finally cried in a choked breath.

Somewhere beneath the frantic beating of my own heart, I heard Ceres whisper the sweetest words. "We love you."

No. No, it's too early for that. Too early, I wanted to say, but my body had other plans. Minutes later, when the strength returned to my body, I realized they'd each settled on a side of me. Tommy held one arm securely around my waist and Ceres nestled against my front.

"That was... wow," I breathed.

Eventually, we split to shower and freshen up. I tossed on one of Tommy's oversized tees and checked my cell phone for any missed calls. None. Jamie was probably at the zoo with his grandparents by now. It was nonstop activity whenever he visited.

I returned to the lovebirds to find them arguing over the shower space. Tommy had on fresh sweats and Ceres wore yoga pants and a tank top.

"He's so cheap, Emma. I've been bothering him for two years about installing bigger showers in these bathrooms."

"Three of us showering together should give him incentive then," I retorted.

Tommy's intrigued expression made us both laugh.

We divided the household tasks and split to go our separate ways. I would make breakfast while they picked up the mess from the party.

"I wish I'd known the both of you planned to seduce me. I would have blown these candles out on my way up," I heard him muttering from the entry way. They had a big house, but the acoustics carried his voice into the kitchen. Giggling as a big smile spread over my face, I crept to the kitchen doorway and plotted a sneak attack.

"What were you thinking, Tommy? We agreed we would tell her first."

I listened to the raw urgency in his voice, an apology in every word. "I couldn't help myself. It just took over," he argued with her. "I'll tell her, okay? I planned to after lunch."

"We'll both tell her," Ceres whispered. "But what if we scare her off?"

The rotating fan tousled my hair. Ceres must have turned them on to help cool their giant house.

"Then that's the risk we—" Tommy abruptly ended his sentence. His shoulders tensed.

I shouldn't be eavesdropping on them, I thought while stepping back.

"It's okay, Em. I know you're there," he said.

"What's going on, guys? Are you talking about me?" Anxiety rolled through my belly as I entered the room. I joined the two who appeared sheepish and apologetic, like they had been caught in the wrong instead of me.

"We've been keeping something secret from you, Em. It's just… It's a big secret, okay? It's not only our secret, either. If you told, it would affect a lot of good people and cause them trouble."

"Huh? Guys, you can trust me."

"Showing you is easier than talking about it," Tommy said. He pushed his sweats down from his hips and stepped out of them.

"Uh. What you look like naked isn't much of a secret anymore. Why are you undressing?"

"You'll see," Ceres replied. She stripped down, too.

I opened my mouth to make a witty retort then lost my ability to breathe. Ceres and Tommy contorted before me as fur rapidly spread over their bodies. They shrank and fell to all fours in the span of two heartbeats. Two wolves stood in their place.

I stumbled back and hit the wall, staring at them with wide eyes. Adrenaline released into my veins and sent my heart to thumping wildly. I couldn't breathe.

My mind reeled with a dozen stories passed down through the Potawatomi oral traditions. During my youth, my grandfather had fascinated me with stories of Chibiabos, the drowned wolf spirit and god of the Underworld. Thomas may as well have been him in the flesh.

"I can't…" They were breathtaking. Ceres approached me first and nudged my hand with her head. Unusual green eyes gazed up at me from her lupine face. Thomas was next, blue-eyed and bold enough to press his muzzle against my lower tummy. His eyes closed as I ran my fingers over his charcoal ears.

"You're both beautiful," I whispered.

Fur vanished, giving way to flesh and hair as the two shifted back into their human skins. Ceres' pale limbs wrapped around me and Tommy's uncertain face filled my vision over her shoulder.

"I can't believe… you're both so pretty."

"You're not freaked out?" Tommy hesitated to touch me. Something about his reluctance made my stomach queasy. I stroked Ceres' hair in an effort to soothe my frazzled nerves.

"No. I'm not. You're… holy shit. You're the wolves from my yard! You're the wolf Jamie pet in the yard! You hugged me!"

Thomas smiled and nodded. "Yeah, that was me. I saw him outside and went up to him. He was brave about it, convinced I was some wolf god your father told him about."

"I was terrified at first, I won't lie."

Ceres pulled back, her smile shy. "We'd never hurt, Jaime. I promise."

"I know."

"Okay. That's one confession down," Tommy said. "I have one more."

"Is it scarier than you turning into wolves?"

"Possibly," he said.

"Do you remember when I asked you about soulmates, Emma?"

I raised my brows at Ceres and nodded. "I do."

"You're ours," Tommy said. "It happens when someone like me is turned, and not born a wolf. You were the soulmate I would have if I were human."

"And I'm the one his wolf chose," Ceres explained.

Soulmates. The idea seemed more bizarre than their shapechanging. "So, what's the other confession?"

"My wolf claimed you while we were having sex and bound our souls as mates."

"Excuse me?" My brows shot up along with my voice.

"If you really don't want it, it'll fade away on its own," Thomas said. His quiet voice lacked emotion. "In a couple weeks. A month at the most."

"What the hell does that mean? You're not telling me what it does. Soul *bonding*?" My voice pitched high with disbelief. All of my life, my tribe had always convinced me there were magical things in this world and that shapechangers walked among humans. I could accept their werewolf secret.

"It means I'm yours for as long as we're bonded. We will always love you, and we'll never want anyone else. It means part of us has been branded into your soul and any shifter will know we belong together."

"You marked me like property? You didn't think to ask me first before you... whatever you did?" I backed away from them both.

Tommy reached out to touch my shoulder. "Emma, please." I jerked back from him. "I couldn't ask. Once the wolf takes over, it's hard to stop anything from happening. And I've been resisting the urge for weeks now."

"Let her go, Tommy. She needs time."

"But—"

"Just let her go! We fucked up, okay?" Tears streaked Ceres' cheeks. "I'm sorry. I knew he was doing it and I didn't stop him."

I sighed. I wanted to stalk out the door and never look back, but I couldn't walk away. Another glance at my two lovers showed Ceres hiding her face against Tommy's shoulder. My best friend's tears drew out my protective nature and brought me back to them.

"Don't cry. I never said I'm going to leave. I'm mad, but there isn't anything that can make me leave now."

"Thank God. I was so, so scared you'd be upset with us," Ceres whispered. She flew into my arms and hugged me tight then Tommy enfolded us both in his embrace.

"I hope this means that I don't have to allow Jamie to have a dog now…"

We all shared a needed laugh and right then I knew — everything was going to be okay.

CHAPTER 16

~THOMAS~

Telling the truth to Emma came as a relief. Ceres and I planned to take things slow by introducing her to the rest of our world one small step at a time. A single phone call from Argus changed all that.

"Thomas, we need you at the estate."

"When do you need me there, Argus? Celebrated my birthday and I'm not even dressed for the day yet." Ceres ran her fingers down the inside of my thigh. I swatted her hand then Emma's when she skimmed down my abs. Both girls tittered. Emma had already gone home to fetch an outfit for a night out on the town. The dress was draped over Ceres' vanity chair.

"I apologize for the timing," Argus told me, "but we need you now, son. The final fight has been set for sundown."

"We'll be there with a plus one," I told him. Ceres kissed my bare chest, her long hair tickling my hip in passing.

"Plus one?"

"You'll see when we get there." I stole a glance at Emma. She feigned innocence, but it was hard to hold a phone conversation with two devilish minxes playing cock tease.

I ended the call then turned to the women. They flanked me on each side, as bubbly as they were insatiable. We'd planned to head into the city to catch a show for the evening.

"Are we going somewhere?" Emma nibbled my collarbone

"To a fight."

Ceres pouted. "But, but I got us special tickets to the—"

"I know," I sighed. "But your dad's the boss."

"What's going on? What do you mean we're going to a fight?"

A wrinkle furrowed Emma's brow, so I reached up and smoothed it away. "Yeah. I'm going to fight another member of my pack, and you get to watch."

"Should I dress nice?" Emma asked.

I laughed at her bewildered expression. "Baby, they're wolves. You're welcome to show up in only a pair of sandals if you want. No one's going to care."

An hour and a half later we joined the pack behind the Prescott's vast home. As we left my truck and made our way around to the rear of the house, Emma marveled over the many shy omegas approaching to welcome her. She was fearless, my proud human beauty becoming the subject of wonder for them as well.

"A third bondmate? That's unusual," Hector commented as he greeted her. "But no less pleasing to discover, Emma. Glad to see you again."

"I *know* you. I've met you in town," Emma gaped. "You teach at Jamie's school."

"Guilty as charged."

"See?" I grinned and kissed Emma's dimple. "We're all around."

"It's nice to meet you again," Daphne said. "As part of our family now."

The rest of the betas made respectful introductions to our third mate, one by one, and sometimes in pairs. Those on two legs took her by the hand or embraced her as a sister.

Argus' piercing howl rang through the evening air, signaling the time for my battle.

"C'mon, Em, we can watch him from the sidelines. It's our right as mates, so we'll stand right there," Ceres told her.

"And watch him win," Emma said, surety in her voice. I loved her all the more for her belief in me.

All three of us moved through the gardens out to the wide open yard. Argus and Vesta waited side by side. Their marriage had ended, officially in the process of legal divorce proceedings, but they still served as pack leaders.

"Honestly, Thomas? A human?" Jason approached us and raked his eyes over Emma. To her credit, she didn't shrink behind me. "You really are a homegrown freak. The Alpha's daughter wasn't enough for you so you had to go back to your chunky roots?"

A snarl bubbled from my throat, but Ceres stepped between us with a palm placed over my chest.

"Ignore him," she murmured low. "He's trying to piss you off. Make you lose focus."

"We have faith in you, Tommy," Emma whispered against my cheek. Ceres kissed the other.

"Go beat his ass."

My mates took my clothes from me after I stripped. The Alphas stood in the makeshift ring, a circle of packed dirt about twenty yards in diameter with heavy rocks bordering the edge. I stepped into the center as a wolf to await their command.

"You've both come a long way to get here, and I want you to know that no matter what's happened or what comes next, I'm proud of your accomplishments," Argus said. His words touched me, but the asshole to my right only smirked before turning to his wolf form.

"We will not call a winner. This fight ends when one of you submits to the other."

Jason and I faced off after the two leaders cleared the ring. My eyes flicked between Argus and my opponent, then swept to the sidelines where the girls watched.

I couldn't let them down.

When Argus gave the signal, we both rushed forward. Jason went for my throat but I twisted my body to roll with the attack. His claws skimmed harmlessly over my thick pelt. Snarling, we snapped with our teeth and rose onto our hind legs, each of us sustaining a bite to the shoulder. He didn't let go, and neither did I. I had to bear through the pain and outlast him.

I could almost hear his voice in my head. Taunting me, harassing the fuck out of me like he did when we were teens. The pain was excruciating, as was the fear of him ripping out my throat. Every time I moved, his jaws squeezed a little harder until I yelped in pain.

I won't lose this way. I scraped at him with my paws until one of my claws hit a sweet spot and caught in his nose. He jerked back and let go, granting me a split second to roll onto my feet. I ducked away, prancing to the side in time to evade his next attack.

My teeth caught him in the ear, tearing through fur and tough skin. He yelped in surprise and ripped away from my teeth to bite my foreleg. Crushing pain radiated through the bone and blood stained his muzzle. Unable to hold weight on the broken limb anymore, I leapt to the side on three legs and defended my flank from his lunge. We clashed, biting, snapping and growling.

Jason's impregnable defense kept me at bay, and on three legs I had little hope. We circled around each other, baring our teeth, then he dove for me.

"Tommy!" Emma's shriek pierced the air.

Guarding my throat, I turned my head and rolled with Jason. We hit the dirt, but I used his heavier weight to my advantage and let it carry us forward. My opponent thumped to the ground beneath me, caught off guard by my decision to allow him the upper hand. My back claws struck his belly then I sank my teeth into his neck and refused to let go. All the while he never stopped kicking at me with his strong legs. He nearly forced me off until I clamped down harder.

I heard the girls screaming from the sidelines. Emma's encouraging cry and Ceres calling out for me to win. Dizzy from blood loss, I nearly stumbled and surrendered my hold.

Can't. Gotta hold on. Just a moment longer.

Jason weakened beneath me and his struggles diminished as I caught my second wind. Without a chance of escaping me, Jason whimpered in defeat and curled his paws against his chest.

"Kill him, Thomas."

I blinked up to see Argus and Vesta standing above us. As I raised my mouth from Jason's neck, the stunned wolf beneath me jerked his head toward our Alpha, too.

"He's lost and submitted. Vesta and I agreed prior to the fight that the loser is no longer welcome to remain a part of either pack.

A hush fell over the crowd of onlookers. Ceres' furious face turned toward her parents before she moved as if she intended to charge the ring. Emma's arms encircled her waist and held her back.

"What if Thomas had lost, Daddy?" she demanded.

"Then his life would be forfeit as well," Argus said.

Vesta glowered at her husband. Her failure to contradict him could only mean two things: it was true, and had her boy toy won, she'd have stood by and let him kill me.

"If you want to gain your title, you will kill him, Thomas," Argus commanded.

I stepped back from the fallen wolf and assumed human shape. Blood trickled down my arm, dripping from my fingertips to the ground below. "No. I won't murder him while he's defenseless. He lost to me and that's the end of it."

"Is that your final decision, Thomas?" Vesta asked. Her surprised features were both desperately relieved and awestruck.

"I won't do it."

"Then it's agreed, Argus. Thomas will be the leader of the new pack." The woman turned away from me and strode from the ring on her high heels. She didn't look back.

"I... what the fuck just happened?"

"That was your final test, Thomas. The test of mercy. You've proven time and again that you possess the qualities desired in a pack leader. You'll protect the ones you love with your strength and your cunning, but most importantly, you'll know when to show mercy to those who may not deserve it." His eyes drifted toward Jason.

Jason rose to his feet and rubbed his neck where I'd gripped him. The skin was broken but far from a mortal injury. "Thanks, man. I don't..." He sighed and glanced at Vesta. She wouldn't return his look. Her cheeks were flushed with shame.

"You wouldn't have spared me. I know."

There was too much bad blood between us for Jason and me to ever become friends, but I didn't miss the gratitude in his eyes. I turned away from him to see my girls racing across the dusty ground to meet me.

"You did it. I knew you could!" Ceres hugged me tight, trembling in relief and taking care to avoid my injuries. Emma embraced me from behind and peppered my shoulder in kisses. Neither woman cared that I was a sweaty mess.

"Win or fail, I'd love you no less, but I am so, so proud of you," Emma whispered against my ear.

Ceres mirrored our mate's sentiment in my other ear. She'd always believed in me ever since we were kids, and now with both phenomenal women in my arms, I believed in myself, too.

CHAPTER 17

ONE YEAR LATER

~EMMA~

"I can't believe Argus had this place built for us. It's huge. We could fit four more families in here."

As a mating gift, Argus had constructed a home away from Atropos where we could live in privacy. It took time to establish a new pack, and even longer to acquire the immense property required for our wolves to live in peace.

After the fight last summer, Jason and Vesta left Texas, heading north to greener pastures. Argus had taken the change in stride and welcomed Jamie and I with open arms.

"An Alpha needs a lot of land to house his pack," Ceres said. "One day, we're going to have omegas of our own. Plus when other groups come through we'll offer our hospitality."

"Dragons, wolves, bears…" I peeked out of the window into the front yard where Thomas ran with a smaller wolf. They were a matching pair, black coats gleaming beneath the summer sun. The pup pounced the larger wolf who rolled over in submission, allowing his junior to gain the upper hand. Jamie didn't refer to Thomas as his stepfather — he called him Dad. I blinked away tears as I watched them.

"Eagles, too," Ceres added with cheer, breaking me out of my thoughts. "I can't wait for you to meet my Uncle Ian."

"Your dad has an eagle for a brother?"

"Well no, they're not related. Just *really* tight friends," she explained. "He's my godfather and you'll love him. He's always away though, with the military. But trust me, he won't miss the wedding once I get the announcements out."

I laughed at her chagrined expression. We'd changed our minds about the invitation styles three times.

"Look at them out there. Jamie looks so happy."

"He reminds me of Thomas after I turned him."

"I'm glad Jamie has him to help through the changes. And that he has a healthier life." When a severe asthma attack threatened to take my son away from me two months ago, I decided then to let Ceres bite him under the full moon. Tommy and Ceres extended the same offer to me, but I declined.

"Are you really sure that you don't want to join us, Em?"

I shook my head and smiled. "I'm sure. This is me. I'm human, and I like being human." I gestured to the scene beyond the window. "You, Tommy, and Jamie were meant for this, and I'm happy enough to be part of your world. Maybe I'll change my mind one day, but right now, I like being *me*. No. I love being me," I clarified.

Ceres nodded. "Okay." Her lips touched mine in a gentle kiss then we laced our fingers together. "There's no expiration date on that offer."

"I know." We kissed again, tender, brief and sweet.

"So, anyway. I have something for you to see." Clearing her throat, Ceres nudged a piece of paper across the counter. I glanced down at the hand drawn designs of twining vines and small blossoms. All three complementary tattoos were intended as wedding band substitutes. The one for Thomas appeared more masculine.

"It's perfect," I whispered, my heart swelling. "Ceres, these are perfect. When can we go get them?"

"Tommy set up the appointments for tomorrow at the tattoo parlor while Dad takes Jamie out for a practice hunt with the omegas."

A joyous squeal bubbled up from my throat as I pulled Ceres into my embrace. She was my girl and Tommy was my guy. Fate had thrust us together as one happy family.

And I wouldn't have it any other way.

ABOUT THE AUTHOR

VIENNE SAVAGE enjoys writing as an outlet for her creativity. She is a video gamer by nature and enjoys watching movies and reading novels by Stephen King, Mary Higgins Clark, Scott Lynch, Mercedes Lackey, Tolkien, and Michael Crichton among others. Vivienne currently lives in Texas with her two children.